My
Favorite
Girl

Playing Favorites, book 0.5

SKYLA SUMMERS

My Favorite Girl
Copyright © 2024 by Eliza Luckey

Contact Information: www.skylasummers.com

ISBN: 978-0-6455663-5-2 (paperback)

Cover Designer: Books and Moods
Editor: MK Books Editing

BOOKS BY SKYLA SUMMERS

Celebrity Fake Dating series

Fake Dating Adrian Hunter

Fake Dating Zac Delavin

Fake Dating Daxton Hawk

Playing Favorites series

My Favorite Girl (prequel novella)

My Favorite Sin (book 1)

A word from Skyla

My Favorite Girl is **book 0.5** in the Playing Favorites series. It is a **prequel novella** to My Favorite Sin.

This novella provides a glimpse into Dan and Ally's teen years and their complicated step sibling dynamic. It ends on a cliffhanger. **Their happy ever after takes place in book 1, My Favorite Sin**.

Sensitive topics in My Favorite Girl include social anxiety and panic attacks. Mention of domestic violence, bullying, and parental death.

Okay, enough talk and let's get to the good stuff. Happy reading!
Skyla xoxo

For all the well behaved girls who like being praised and told they're a good girl when doing the wrong thing.

The First Year

Innocence

Chapter 1

Dan

Thursday, May 13

<small>MY FATHER'S NEW GIRLFRIEND</small>

If there's one benefit to being a Blackwood, it's how eager every girl is to ride my dick.

There's a girl in my bed, straddling my thighs. We met last night at my friend's seventeenth. She's pretty. Nice eyes and with dark hair that sits around her shoulders. Perky tits. She couldn't wait to whip off her bra and show me. I don't know a thing about her other than her name is Monique.

She doesn't care. They never do.

They're always just excited to run off and tell their friends they've slept with a Blackwood.

I pull her panties to the side and bring her hips in line with mine.

"Dan." My father knocks on my bedroom door and I instantly lose the hard-on. For fuck's sake. The one time the man chooses to come back to the penthouse and take an interest in me has to be right now, midnight on a random Thursday, when he's ordinarily off with his new girlfriend.

Monique gasps. "Is that your dad?" Her confidence vanishes and she's covering herself with my bedsheet.

"The door is locked," I reassure her. "Ignore him. He'll disappear in a second."

"Dan." The knocking turns impatient, matching the tone of my father's voice. "I know you're in there. We need to talk."

"I'm busy," I shout back.

Monique climbs off me. "Your dad sounds kind of mad. Maybe I should get dressed."

I force down my frustration and pull on a pair of track pants. "No, just... hang out in the bathroom while I get rid of him."

She scurries off into my adjoining bathroom, the knocking continuing.

"What do you want?" I answer the door.

My father, always in a designer suit and with his dark hair never a strand out of place, looks down at my bare chest then past me to my unmade bed. Monique is out of sight but he's wise enough to know I have a girl in here with me. I have three older brothers; he knows what we're like and doesn't care. Probably because he's led with such a fine example, having fucked half the women in this city without knowing their names. At least I took the time to learn Monique's.

"Dan, I'd like to have a serious discussion with you about Amabella. Get dressed and meet me in the living room."

His girlfriend. I've never met her, but then again, I've never met any of the women he sleeps with. I've never known their names unless I saw it online. The paparazzi love following my father. He's a socialite and one of the wealthiest bachelors in New York City, along with having built a hotel empire.

Amabella is the first woman he's kept around for longer than a month and told me and my brothers about. He says she's a seating hostess at a restaurant here on the Upper East Side. I'm not judging the lady by her career but she seems beneath his standards, considering I've only known him to sleep with models.

"I have a guest in my bathroom," I tell him. "We can talk later."

His jaw tics, frustrated by my answer. The two of us can't go five minutes without arguing. Tonight, however, he doesn't push back.

He wants something from me.

"We can talk here," he says. "I'll make this quick. I'd like you to meet Amabella—"

"I don't need to meet the women you sleep with."

"Dan." My name is curt out of his lips. A warning. "Amabella is different. I'm serious about her. Perhaps I'm getting ahead of myself, but I can see myself marrying her. Not without the approval of you and your brothers, of course. It's important that you feel comfortable with the addition to our family."

My eyebrows draw together with disbelief over every word that's left my father's mouth. Since when has he ever cared about our family? The man had nannies raising me and my older brothers from the day I was born. The way he coped with the death of our mother was to throw himself into work and stick his dick in everything that moved. I understand he needed time to grieve, but not sixteen years. Now he wants us to act like a family? What a joke.

"You can marry whoever you want. I don't care and I don't want to be a part of it."

"Dan, you *will* be a part of it. I'd like her to move in here. I want to focus on family and less on work. From now on, you'll be seeing a lot more of me around here, whether you like it or not."

Fuck this shit. I push the door shut, but he juts an arm out, holding the door open.

"What do I have to do to make you cooperate with me? Amabella is an important part of my life, and I will not have your attitude ruin my relationship with her."

"There's nothing—"

"Felix tells me you're about to get your driver's license. I'll buy you a car. Any car you want if it means you'll work with me."

The nerve of this man. Now he's bribing me?

But the proposition makes me pause. *Any* car? It's not an empty promise. My father has always thrown money around to fix his problems.

"Fine." I can play along to get what I want. Doesn't mean I have to be genuine toward my father and his new girlfriend.

"Thank you. You and I will be having lunch with Amabella this Saturday."

I lift a brow. "Just us? No Felix, Tyler, or Killian?"

He straightens the lapels of his jacket. "I'd like to introduce you and your brothers to Amabella individually. Less chance for chaos."

"Can't wait." My voice drags over each word. My brothers would have made this lunch bearable.

I go to close the door again, but he holds it open. "One more thing, Dan. Amabella has a daughter named Ally. She's a year younger than you and will be joining us for the lunch. She's a quiet girl and doesn't have many friends. You'll be welcoming to Ally as well, understood?"

Jesus fuck. Fine. Anything to get this conversation over with. "Sure. Me and the daughter, best friends. Are we done here?"

My dad nods and leaves. I'll be asking for a Ferrari after all this is over.

Chapter 2

Dan

"Remember, best behavior," my father mutters like I'm five years old as we wait for his girlfriend to answer her front door.

She lives at The Hawk Grand Hotel on the Upper East Side, a few streets away from us. When I asked why she lives in a hotel, I got some cryptic response about the girlfriend having a rough past, and that she's cousins with Daxton Hawk, the guy who owns this hotel, and he housed her here to help out.

Along with my best behavior, my father insisted I wear a suit to set a good impression. He's nervous about today's lunch with the girlfriend and her daughter, afraid I'll mention something embarrassing about his fabulous parenting skills. I'll let him sweat, but I'm not an idiot. I want that car.

The door opens, and a woman in her early thirties, at least ten years younger than my father, smiles at me. This is Amabella, I suppose. She's beautiful, with an elegance his usual women don't possess. Amabella has long, blond hair and is wearing a floral dress fit for this time of year as we grow closer to summer.

She doesn't spare a glance at my father before pulling me into a hug. "Dan, I am *so* thrilled to meet you. Your father has told me so many wonderful things about you." All lies from him, I'm sure. The little he does know about me, he doesn't like.

The woman's warm and excitable nature is unexpected, and before I can reciprocate any kind of response, she laughs and pulls back, holding me by the shoulders. "Sorry, I should have introduced myself first. You're probably freaking out. I'm Amabella."

"It's nice to officially meet you."

Only now does Amabella turn to my father. She pecks him on the lips, and they exchange a few cutesy words. I look away, disturbed by the sight of my father smiling against her mouth.

"Please, come inside," Amabella says to us. "Our lunch reservations at the restaurant downstairs aren't for another forty minutes."

We follow her through the front door to a small but sophisticated apartment. The living room and kitchen are combined in an open floor plan, with a balcony to the side.

Amabella stands with Dad near the couch and calls out, "Ally, honey, Josh and Dan are here."

Right. The daughter I have to play nice with.

A door opens somewhere behind me, followed by a quiet voice. "Hi."

I turn to the timid sound. The moment I see our

company, a jolt of heat shoots from my chest all the way down to my dick.

This is the daughter?

I don't know what I was expecting but it wasn't this.

I'm staring at something from another world. The most delicate and beautiful creature who looks like she's just stepped out of a fairy garden. She has the palest skin and ice-blond hair draped by her waist in soft curls. A pink satin ribbon sits in her hair and she's wearing a white lacy dress with a lilac knit cardigan.

The girl looks at me with the most mesmerizing blue eyes that make me forget how to talk. I didn't realize I have a type, but I do and it's this girl. I only hold her attention for a second at most before her gaze flicks away and drops to the ground. The slight smile she greeted me with vanishes and her hands clench by her sides.

"Dan." There's a warning in my father's voice which brings me back to reality, alerting me that I've been staring in silence for far too long.

Somehow, I find it within me to speak in a casual manner. "Hey, Ally, nice to meet you."

"You too. Hi, Josh." Her voice is so quiet I barely hear it. She hugs my father, and I watch the interaction between the two, shocked at how comfortable they are with each other, like she's his own daughter. I suppose he spends a lot of time here with Amabella and Ally, considering he's never home.

"Would anyone like a drink?" Amabella asks.

"I'll serve it," Ally says in that quiet voice again, stuttering over her words. Her face turns a shade of pink, I have no clue why, and she pivots on her heels, heading to the kitchen.

"I'll help you." The words leave my mouth before I know what I'm saying.

I gave Dad my word I would be welcoming, but this has nothing to do with that promise. I don't know what's gotten into me. I'm *never* like this with girls. I'm not sure if I want to fuck her or follow her around like a puppy dog, earning her love and affection. Both options. Maybe more so the latter.

My brothers would have the biggest laugh of their life if they saw me like this over a girl. They wouldn't recognize me. I don't recognize myself.

"It's o-okay," Ally stutters again. "You don't need to help—"

"Where are the glasses kept?"

Amabella smiles, looking between me and Ally with approval, then at my dad with a silent squee of excitement, like she's pleased I've taken an interest in her daughter.

"Thanks, Dan," Amabella says, leading my father outside by the hand. "Josh and I will be waiting on the balcony."

Without another word, Ally busies herself in the kitchen, grabbing a jug of what looks like homemade lemonade from the fridge. Next, she opens an overhead cabinet where the glasses are stored. The majority of glasses must be in the dishwasher, because the cabinet is mostly empty other than a few glasses tucked at the back. Ally reaches up on her toes, her dress riding up her thighs as she struggles to reach.

I enjoy the sight for a few seconds, visualizing what she'd look like naked and in my bed. Not wanting to be caught staring, I step up beside her, reaching the glasses with ease. She's so tiny, it's adorable. This close, she smells like strawberries and candy and everything sweet.

Her cheeks form a rosy hue as she looks at my chest and the shortened distance I've placed between us. I make her nervous. I wonder how much this girl knows about me, being a Blackwood. If she's seen the usual shit about me and my brothers online—the partying, girls, and alcohol—she's probably already made her assumptions.

I hand her the glasses. She offers me a tight smile in return before silently pouring the lemonade. Whatever her assumptions are, I need to change her opinion of me.

I lean against the kitchen counter. "Nice shoes." I'm only now realizing she's wearing Converse, matching the lilac of her cardigan, the only thing that lets me know she's from this world.

She looks down at her feet before muttering, "Is that a joke?"

"No." I pause, muddled over her question and why she thinks I'm joking. "I like them and the contrast with your outfit."

Ally presses her lips together, deep in thought, almost looking offended by my comment. She resumes pouring the drinks in silence.

"Did I say something wrong?"

"The girls at school tease me for how I dress. I can't tell if you're being sarcastic."

I fold my arms, laughing beneath my breath. "The girls at school are jealous. Trust me."

Dad said Ally attends an all-girls school and that she doesn't have many friends. I'm sure I'm not supposed to know this, but he also mentioned her being bullied. I can say with certainty the bullying would stem from every one of those girls being intimidated by Ally's looks.

"I doubt they're jealous," she mumbles.

From the moment I entered this apartment, every word

that's left Ally's mouth has been filled with shyness. I get it now; her guard is up due to bad experiences.

"My dad tells me you play the piano."

She stops pouring the lemonade to look at me. Her lips twitch with the hint of a smile, and that same heat from the first moment I saw her radiates through me.

"Yes, I play. It's the only thing I *ever* do."

"Can you play something for me right now?"

"Um... really?"

"Yeah, our parents can wait for their drinks. Show me. I hear you're amazing."

"The piano is in my bedroom." The blush returns to her cheeks, and it makes me wonder if she's ever had a guy in her room. Doubtful. She gives off an innocent vibe. I bet she's never had a guy's hands on her body or been kissed.

Oddly, the thought of her innocence is a turn on. I don't fuck around with inexperienced girls. There's no time since I'm only with them for a night. They expect romance and dates and to take things slow. I'm not that kind of guy.

Where Ally is concerned, I have time. I have all the time in the world. I'm being ruled by my dick, but the thought of *this* girl being untouched is far too tempting. I don't know why. Maybe it has something to do with her being the daughter of my father's girlfriend. I told him I would behave around Ally, but behaving is the last thing I want to do.

"Do you like Mozart?" she asks.

"Couldn't name a single song by him."

"You'd know many by him if you heard them."

Each time she speaks, it's filled with more confidence now that we're discussing a passion of hers. My father said Ally isn't shy at all once you get her talking about music. It's cute, seeing her like this compared to the timid girl from a couple of minutes ago. She doesn't have many friends to share this passion with? She can share it with me all she wants.

"My husband's music is very well renowned," she continues.

I'm confused for a moment until Ally chuckles, and fuck, the sound of her soft laughter makes my dick twitch. She's making a joke, I guess. Her sense of humor is a little unusual, but I like it.

"You got any other husbands? Beethoven? Bach?" I try to list off a few other classical composers, but my knowledge of that era isn't great.

"I have *so* many husbands. Come on, I'll show you."

I follow Ally to her bedroom, and just like the girl herself, her room is like stepping into another time and world. Everything is covered in ruffles and lace and the prettiest of ribbons. It's all pastels and light colors. A white piano sits upright against the wall, and along the top are small sculptures of composers.

Her eyes widen the tiniest bit when I sit on her bed. Ally stares at me and licks her lips, her gaze heating me to the core. She's such a sweet looking girl, but I can see in her eyes that she's thinking about sex. How the hell does she have this effect over me, to make me insanely turned on over something as simple as sitting on a girl's bed?

My oldest brother Felix once told me it's the innocent looking girls you have to watch out for, that they're the most freaky between the bedsheets.

Ally glances away and opens the piano lid. I'm about to ask if she'd prefer I sit somewhere else, but she dives into her song, playing the piano with such fluency it feels like I'm attending a concert.

My God, she's beautiful when she plays. Her face is

serene, like she's one with the music. Sometimes, she plays with her eyes closed, she's that talented. I wish I was inside her head this very moment, experiencing the passion she clearly feels when playing the piano.

"*That* is Mozart," she says at the end of her short performance. The tune is familiar, one I've heard many times in ads and movies.

"I know the song. My dad wasn't kidding when he said you're an amazing pianist. Can you teach me to play something?"

I don't know why I ask the question. I don't have any interest in playing the piano. But there's a light in her eyes that only appeared once we started speaking about music. I don't know much about her, but I like seeing that light. I want this girl to smile at me, talk to me non-stop, and let me into her inner circle. Then I want to take her back to my bed and I don't want her to leave. I want to test this theory Felix claims about innocent looking girls.

Ally rubs the back of her neck, seeming confused by my question. "You mean teach you something right now or give you lessons?"

Fuck, the latter is an even better suggestion. "Give me lessons."

"Okay, I guess. How often should we—"

"A few times a week."

She stands up, closes the piano lid, and smiles. "That sounds fun. I'd like that."

Not as much as me, Ally, trust me.

Chapter 3

Ally

Nine days later, Monday, May 23

I HAVE A FRIEND. A *REALLY* HANDSOME FRIEND

The school day finishes and I leave the building, keeping my head down as I walk through a crowd of girls, minding my own business while tapping the notes of *Clair de lune* against my thighs.

"Ally."

My feet come to a dead stop, my heart thumping at the deep, smooth voice speaking my name. I look up from the ground, my eyes catching on him in disbelief.

Dan Blackwood is standing at my school gates, grinning at me.

His back is slumped against the stone gatepost and his hands are in the pockets of his uniform. He's wearing black Ray Ban sunglasses, such a rich-boy look, and when he removes them, revealing his dark eyes upon me, my stomach does a little flip. My temperature rises. I hope he can't see the heat in my cheeks, but I'm doubtful. Dan is very handsome and my body does a terrible job at hiding that I think so.

All the Blackwood boys are gorgeous. I looked them up when Mom first told me she was dating Josh. There's Killian, who's a year older than Dan. Then the two eldest who no longer live at home—Tyler at twenty, and Felix is twenty-one. They all look like the kind of guy my father wouldn't let me anywhere near, if I had a father. The brothers are dangerously beautiful, like they could break a girl's heart with one kiss.

Maybe that's why after two months of Josh dating my mother and spending countless hours with the two of us, he's only just come around to the idea of introducing me to Dan. I don't know what it's like to have a father, but Josh plays the role well whenever he visits, and I'm growing attached to having him around.

Dan might be the most dangerous of all his brothers. The way he's grinning at me right now in the school grounds does something to my body I've never experienced before. It makes my stomach tight, but in a good way, like I never want him to stop looking at me. He has this boyish charm to him, the way his dark hair is ruffled and how he wears his uniform undone at the collar, with the tie loose and the white sleeves rolled up to his elbows.

I step up to him at the gate, smiling a little, trying to hide how pleased I am to see him. "What are you doing here?"

"Missed you. Thought we could study together this afternoon."

It's been just over a week since we first met, and we've already seen each other five times. He visits my apartment with his father, for piano lessons, dinner, movies, anything, really. I asked Dan what kind of things he's into, and the answer was poker, courtesy of his oldest brother Felix teaching him the game a year ago, against Josh's wishes, I'm sure.

Dan insists he'll teach me how to play. When I told him I'm too young, he laughed at me. Not in the rude way I experience from the girls at school, but as if he thought my answer was adorable.

He has this way of talking to me, always holding eye contact, and sounding amused, like he's flirting with me. That's how he spoke to me when I turned down the poker offer. There's no difference right now as he tells me he missed me. I assume he's just a flirt and talks to every girl like this, so I try not to flatter myself.

"Hey, Ally." Two girls in my class approach me, Nicole and Rachel, who I once thought were my friends. They haven't spoken to me in months. All I receive from them these days is cruel laughter and whispers. "Can you introduce us to your friend?" Nicole asks.

Of course they're playing nice now that I'm seen with a Blackwood. The Blackwood name is prestigious in this city, considering the wealth and reputation Josh has earned through his hotel business. He's also a philanthropist. A very admirable man, though Dan has dropped hints that lead me to believe he feels differently about his father. The media follows Josh around like he's a celebrity. They follow his sons too, though all the boys seem to do is cause scandal with their constant partying.

I quietly introduce Nicole and Rachel to Dan, knowing their behavior toward me at school will only worsen if I go against their wishes.

They offer Dan big smiles and lots of girlish laughter.

"We heard you talking about studying this afternoon," Nicole says. "Can we join?"

"I should be getting home," I mutter to the three of them. Let them have Dan. Whatever. If it makes my life easier at school, I'll take it. They're probably the kind of girls he's into anyway. Big breasts. Popular. Sexual. I've overheard them talk about all the guys they get with. They wear tons of makeup to school and fold their uniform waistbands to make their skirts shorter, leaving little to be imagined.

I step by them, but Dan's finger hooks around mine, his touch hot and unexpected and spreads sparks all over my body. "Afraid not, ladies," he says in a matter-of-fact way. No teasing. No flirting. "I want to get this one alone."

The girls stare at me in shock. Almost as shocked as I am to hear Dan speak those words. He drapes an arm around my shoulders and leads us out to the street.

"You want to get me alone?" I ask, trying to shrug out from beneath his arm as we walk on the city sidewalk, but he chuckles and keeps me in place.

"I had to say some shit to get rid of those girls. But it's the truth. You're so much more fun when it's the two of us and say the weirdest shit I could listen to for hours."

"Like what?" I ask in disbelief that he could possibly think I'm fun. All I ever do is play the piano and talk about music. I have no social skills. People think I'm weird. Maybe I am weird. I've come to accept that.

"Last night when we were having dinner at your place with our parents," he starts, and I don't even have to look at him to know he's grinning. I can hear it in his voice. "I mean, you're cute and all in front of them, talking about Renaissance music. But as soon as they're out of earshot, you blush and tell me the trombone used to be called a sackbut, like it was some dirty word you couldn't say in front of them."

I laugh, covering my face with embarrassment. "You have to admit a sackbut *does* sound like a rude word." And oh my goodness, how can he so casually slip into the conversation that I'm cute. The word came out of his mouth with such ease that I know he only meant it in a friendly way, not for me to be obsessing over it.

As we arrive at a cross intersection, Dan veers us right, instead of in the direction of my apartment. "My mom is expecting me at home," I say.

"So? Text her and tell her you're studying at the public library with me. She loves me."

That's true. I think more than anything, she's thrilled I have a friend, if that's what Dan and I are. He feels like a friend. A really handsome friend who I've visualized kissing on more than one occasion. But I won't share that information with anyone, especially not him. I'm sure he'd laugh at how easily my body responds to the simple touch of his arm on my shoulders or how he hooked his finger with mine a few minutes ago. Those are the kinds of things that stir something deep within my belly, having such limited experience with guys.

Dan isn't on the same playing field. He has *sex* written all over him. I know the kind of guy he is. I'm sure he sees me as just a friend and only takes an interest in me because of our parents.

"And *will* we be studying at the library, or is that a cover up?" I've never lied to my mother before. I don't want to lie to her either. She's my best friend and she's protective of me after everything that happened with her ex-boyfriend.

"Yeah, we'll be at the library."

"Studying?"

He sighs, laughing, and squeezes my shoulders. "Oh, I can see why my dad is so fond of you. Such a role model child, for once. Yes, we'll study."

I open my mouth to respond, closing it again, my muscles stiffening when I see someone across the street take a photo of us. A man with a professional camera.

Dan must sense my discomfort. He follows my gaze, seeing the man. "This your first encounter with paparazzi? Ignore them. That's what I always do."

"Kind of hard to ignore when I haven't grown up in the world of fame. I guess it's something I'll need to get used to now that our parents are dating, but I don't think I'll like the attention."

Dan switches positions, stepping to the other side of me, shielding me from view with his body. "Better?"

"Maybe a little. Thank you."

It's not long before we arrive at the library, the quiet atmosphere and escape from the cameraman a relief. Dan leads me to an area at the back, where people are still scattered around, sitting at tables and searching through the stacks, but where we have a little more freedom to talk. We settle at a table and sit opposite each other, with me flipping through an art history textbook and Dan advanced mathematics. He must be good with numbers, which is the complete opposite to how my creative brain works.

"So..." Dan murmurs after a few minutes of our studies. "What was with you and those girls at the school gates?"

I don't look up from my textbook, hoping to brush off the topic. "Oh, um, nothing."

"Didn't seem like nothing. You don't like them?"

"More like they don't like me. I don't really... have any friends at school." I can feel my face turning red at the embarrassing confession. "I don't have friends outside of school either, other than my mom and uncle Daxton."

"I don't see why."

"It's a long story that I've spent years in therapy trying to deal with. I'll spare you the details."

Dan shrugs, focusing on his textbook. "We're friends. I'll listen."

Finally, I look up from my page, liking that he thinks we're friends. He peers up at me and grins, then abandons his textbook and slumps back in his chair with his legs spread wide. Sitting in that position, Dan looks like such a guy. It's kind of hard to concentrate when he looks so good.

My gaze lowers to his dick and I swallow hard. I realize I've been caught staring when he laughs, the sound quiet but smug and making me flustered enough to forget the topic of conversation.

I avert my gaze. "Um... What were we talking about?"

"I asked why you don't have friends."

"Oh. Um... I've got daddy issues, I guess." Jesus. Did I have to state it like that?

"You and me both." He gives a humorless laugh. "Where is your dad?"

"He died when I was a baby."

Dan frowns. "I'm sorry to hear that. My mom died giving birth to me. My dad has always resented me for it."

My mouth opens and closes with shock, not knowing how to respond. "I don't know what to say. That must be so... difficult for you."

"Won't lie, I'm pretty fucked up over it."

A *sorry for your loss* doesn't seem appropriate in this moment. I don't know what does. Surely Josh doesn't resent Dan, but it doesn't feel right for me to comment on that topic either. With my heart pounding, I reach out and place my hand on Dan's as an offer of comfort, relieved when he doesn't pull away.

Dan looks down at our two hands then up at me, his throat working. His fingers curl around mine and give a little squeeze. "I don't talk about her. Ever. Can I hear the rest of your story?"

Respecting his privacy, I continue. "Has Josh told you about my mom's last boyfriend?"

"Me and my dad don't really talk."

I kind of figured things were tense between them. There have been a few snide comments made here and there, from both father and son, but for the most part, they seem pleasant together whenever I'm around.

"Well, my mom was a victim of domestic violence. The last man she dated... I was just a kid when they were together. We lived with him for a few years and he was terrible. He hit her many times. I'm confident he would have..." My voice trembles and my throat restricts. The words are too painful to speak out loud, that he would have killed her if she hadn't found the strength to leave.

From the shock on Dan's face, I get the impression he understands exactly what my silence is hinting at. It feels a little strange sharing these intimate details of my mother's life, but the domestic violence was a part of my life too. Mom's ex never laid his hands on me, but having a front row seat to him abusing my mother has left its scar on me in other ways.

I take a steadying breath. "My therapist says what I witnessed made me retreat into myself. It affected my confidence and social skills. I've dealt with ongoing panic attacks because of the abuse. And, well... I suppose it's impacted my school life. The other girls think I'm too quiet and...

strange, I guess. They've done some pretty terrible things to me."

"Fuck them. Seriously." Dan speaks the words too loud, and with a little too much frustration, earning us glares from nearby people. He squeezes my hand again, controlling his voice this time. "We're friends now. I'll meet you at your school gates every afternoon."

I lick my lips, tingling from the way he looks directly into my eyes. "*Every* afternoon? What about your friends?"

"I see them all day at school. They can live without me in the afternoons."

I retrieve my hand from his and look down at my textbook, though there's no way I can focus on anything but what Dan has suggested. "Don't you have other commitments, like, a girlfriend and stuff?"

"I don't have a girlfriend."

"You have girls, though. I... hear things about you."

Dan laughs, my gaze flicking up to him and seeing his lips tug into a grin. "Yeah, like what?" He folds his arms across his chest, deeply amused, and I blush all over again.

"You're a Blackwood. Do I need to say more?"

"Yeah, I think you do."

I throw my pen at him, laughing. He dodges the attack. "Are you just trying to make me say more dirty things, like sackbut?"

"Yeah, I am." He grins. "You seem innocent. Too innocent."

He's got that right. The way Dan has *sex* written all over him, I'm sure I read as *virgin*.

"You ever been kissed?" he asks.

I frown with terrible memories coming back to me. "Yes. Once."

"What, the guy didn't treat you right or something?"

"Um... the bullying I told you about? At one point, turns out the girls had asked a guy to pretend to be into me. They all thought it would be funny if they dared him to kiss me and caught it on camera."

His brows pinch together. "What the fuck, Ally."

"Yeah." My voice retreats. I grab a pen from my pencil case, twisting it between my fingers as an outlet for my nervous energy. "I don't have a good experience with guys. Even men, after what I witnessed with Mom's ex. That's why I like Josh. He's kind to us and he cares. He treats me like I imagine a dad would treat his daughter." I bite my bottom lip, worrying that I've said the wrong thing. "Sorry if that's hard for you to hear. I know things between you two aren't good."

"Don't apologize. If you like him... That's fine, Ally. It's better than fine. You deserve to feel happy and safe after what you've been through."

His approval makes me smile a little, although there's something that's been playing on my mind, especially after this heavy discussion. "You seriously like hanging out with me? There's no ulterior motive? No prank?"

"No prank, Ally."

My breath turns shallow from the warmth of his eyes upon me.

"I like you," he says.

"But I'm not the kind of girl you normally hang around. I mean, what do you even want with me?"

"I don't know. I like learning about all your husbands and hearing you talk about sackbuts."

I smile, and this time, there's no doubt holding me back. He has that amused look in his eyes again, teasing me, and I think I might be in serious trouble. I like the way he looks at me more than I've ever liked anything before.

Chapter 4

Ally

Three weeks later, Friday, June 15

DAN IS ABOUT TO BECOME MY... STEPBROTHER?

I have a crush. My first real crush and on a guy who actually exists. A guy who texts me every day and walks me home from school. It's been one month since we first met, and every Wednesday afternoon, we visit a 50s style diner and sit across from each other in a booth, sharing a milkshake with two straws. We laugh about TV shows and movies.

During our piano lessons, he asks me to play music for him, and lies back on my bed, watching like he's entranced by my skill. Then he sits beside me on the stool and tries his hardest to copy everything I teach him.

When our parents aren't looking, he teaches me the rules of poker. I'm no good at it and he teases me, yet it's in a fun way I've never experienced before. I like teasing him back. I like when the left side of his mouth curls into a grin. I like the deep sound of his voice and how he speaks my name. How he hugs me each time we say goodbye.

I like everything about Dan Blackwood.

Yet, I'll never take this crush to the next level. Not only because our parents are dating and it would be weird, but because Dan and I are friends. I've been so lonely and miserable for years, but now he's come into my life and I think this is the first time I've ever truly been happy. I like how easy it is to talk to Dan, when normally I can't string a sentence together in front of a guy. I'm not about to ruin any of this by letting my feelings get in the way.

"The tennis courts are down that path." Josh points to our left, giving my mom and me a tour of his summer home in The Hamptons, which he insists is now our home since Mom got time off work and we're spending the entire summer break here with him.

Mansion would be a more accurate description. This is by far the biggest and fanciest place I've ever visited. His property is right on the beach with expansive land and a driveway a mile long. The mansion is elegant, in typical Hamptons style architecture, white with large windows and porches. There's a five-car garage, incredible pool, and the gardens are immaculately groomed. There's even a hedge maze Josh has advised me not to enter alone in case I get lost.

"Do you play tennis, Ally?" Josh asks as we round a corner in the garden, the three of us stopping by a water fountain.

"No. I'd love to learn."

"We'll have to teach you while we're here for the summer."

"Speaking of which, do you know when Dan will be arriving?"

It's early evening and the sun is about to set. The school year finished today, and Josh drove the three of us up here after Mom finished her shift at the restaurant. Dan was meant to come too but was held up with a prior arrangement. As for Josh's other sons, I still haven't met them. Josh invited them to spend the summer with us, but they turned down the invitation.

"Dan should hopefully be arriving soon. He's busy with his brothers," Josh says, which is code for *playing poker*. He tries to hide his displeasure of Dan's absence, along with the reason, but I can tell he's unhappy with Dan's choices.

"Ah, the brothers," Mom sighs, laughing fondly as she weaves her fingers with Josh's.

Unlike me, she's met Killian, Tyler, and Felix, and says they're lovely. When Dan heard her describe them in such a way, he started choking on his drink with laughter.

Despite Dan telling me not to be nervous about meeting them, that they'll love me, I *am* nervous. I don't do well around new people, regardless of my good intentions. My awkward tendencies get interpreted for rudeness, and that's the last thing I want Dan's brothers to think of me.

I dip my fingers into the fountain. "When will I meet your other sons?"

"Soon enough, honey. Are you two hungry?" Josh changes the subject quickly. I don't pry further, curious but respecting his wishes, and instead follow him and my mom inside for dinner.

After we've eaten, we spend the rest of the evening together in the living room, playing board games and laughing, and it feels nice, like we're a real family. Dan texted me earlier in the day telling me he'd be here tonight, but when I still haven't heard from him at ten p.m., I decide to call it a night and go to bed.

The guest bedroom Josh has given me is upstairs and next to where he and my mom are sleeping. Mom won't say it out loud, but I know she's keeping me close by in case I have a panic attack in the middle of the night.

We've narrowed the cause of these panic attacks down to me feeling trapped in uncomfortable social situations that I can't remove myself from. The episodes happen a lot at school. Medication is the only thing that helps. When I was younger, on the rare chance I was ever invited to a sleep-over, the attacks happened there, too. It was embarrassing, having the girls at school witness me like that, then needing my mom to pick me up.

I've learned to control my environment by accepting fewer social invitations. Now, I never get invited anywhere. It's helped the anxiety but has brought on loneliness and an inability to feel normal. I'm sure it only encouraged the bullying. It's a vicious cycle I can't break.

But I've reassured Mom I want to be at Josh's beach house, and it's the truth. It feels like home here, with two loving parents, and I drift to sleep instantly.

The hour is still dark when I wake to a repeated *clinking* sound. I rub my eyes, my phone telling me it's one in the morning. I also have a bunch of missed calls and texts from Dan.

The sound continues, coming from the window in my room. A pebble hits the glass. I open the window, finding Dan in the garden beneath my room.

"Finally." He grins up at me with a black hoodie pulled over his head, his voice not too loud, like he doesn't want to risk waking our parents. "The house is locked and I don't have keys. I've been throwing rocks at all the guest bedrooms, trying to find where you're sleeping. Let's go for a walk on the beach."

"Right now?" I call back, matching his hushed volume.

"Yeah. Why not?"

I look back at my bedroom door, knowing my mom wouldn't approve of me leaving the house at this hour, especially being in a new location and with my history of panic attacks. I'm about to suggest Dan comes inside and we talk in the living room, but a flicker of excitement stirs in my chest at the thought of sneaking out and being truly alone with Dan. I've never snuck out before. I've never *had* anyone to sneak out with. I've never done anything my mother wouldn't approve of, nor have I had the urge to.

But that grin on Dan's face makes me want to do something wrong for once.

"Okay. Let's go to the beach." The words feel electrifying leaving my mouth. I scope the trellis, not wanting to risk waking Mom and Josh if I sneak out the door. "You think I can climb out the window?"

"Yeah. I'll spot you."

My muscles tighten with adrenaline as I hoist myself over the windowsill and cling to the trellis. A cool breeze rolls in from the beach, ruffling my hair and caressing the bare skin on my legs, making me realize I didn't think through this plan at all. I'm not wearing any shoes, my sleep shorts hardly cover my ass, and I don't have a bra beneath this baggy shirt. As an A cup, it's not like I'm in need of much support, but I don't want Dan seeing the points of my nipples.

Too late now. This feeling of excitement that Dan awakens within me is too addictive and I'm not climbing back inside. Taking care with my footing, I descend slowly, making sure not to trample the flowers growing on this trellis. Halfway down, a yelp escapes me as I step on a weak part of wood and the trellis crumbles beneath my feet, leaving me scrambling and clinging to the wall.

"Oh, shit. Are you okay?" Dan whisper-yells.

My feet dig into a crevice on the side of the house, securing my safety, and I let out a much needed breath of relief. A light switches on from within Mom and Josh's bedroom. My stomach twists, knowing if they peer outside, I'll be caught and have a lot of explaining to do. She'll put two and two together, realizing I have a crush on her boyfriend's son, because why else would I sneak out to be with a guy?

I hear my mother's voice, though her words aren't clear. All I know is I need to find a way out of this situation and fast. But when I look down, realizing my climbing path to the ground is gone, I have no clue what to do.

"Jump. I'll catch you."

I peer over my shoulder at Dan. "You can't be serious. It's a long way."

My mother's silhouette appears right on the other side of the curtain, making my pulse thunder in my ears. Time is running out. Any moment now, she'll open the curtains and catch me red-handed. Jumping is my best option, but fear holds me in place.

"It's not that far," Dan says. "Do you trust me?"

"Yes, but I'm still scared to jump the distance. What if I'm too heavy and you drop me?"

"Not going to happen. You're tiny."

"But—"

"Ally, get on the fucking ground already so I can hug you."

My pulse kicks into overdrive, having nothing to do with fear this time. My heart squeezes at the playful way

Dan scolds me and how he wants to hug me. Jumping is worth it, just for that hug.

"Okay. Three, two, one." I let go, my stomach vanishing as I fall through the air.

Strong arms catch me, one beneath my legs, the other at my back, cradling me to his chest. Above us, the window opens. Dan rushes us out of sight, around the corner of the house, saving us just in time from being caught.

"The trellis broke," Josh says from a distance. "Must have been some wild animal climbing it. I'll take care of it in the morning. Let's go back to bed."

"You little rebel." Dan grins at me and I laugh. He holds me for a moment longer than necessary before lowering me to my feet, yet doesn't release me from his arms.

I get that hug I was promised, being lifted off my toes. His warmth spreads through my body and I soak it up, also noticing the scent of alcohol. Though he doesn't seem drunk. On anyone else, I wouldn't like the smell. But with Dan... well, I've already accepted nothing he does will turn me off.

"Fuck, I missed you."

I've never liked swearing, but the way he says *fuck* in that deep, gravelly tone makes me think it could be my new favorite word.

Dan buries his face in my hair, breathing deeply. Sometimes I wonder when he says things like this, if I'm not the only one with a crush. I let myself get carried away with the fantasy, but I'll never ask.

"Sorry it took me so long to get up here," he says. "I got caught up with Killian and Felix, playing poker."

"Did you win?"

"A couple of games." Dan looks down at my body, seeing my pajamas. "Are you cold?"

Before I can answer, he pulls off his hoodie and places it over my head. My arms slip into it with ease. I don't object, the hoodie surrounding me with his warmth and scent.

"How did you get up here?" I ask.

"Felix drove me. He's waiting out in the front with Killian. They want to meet you."

My eyes pop open wide with panic. "Oh... Maybe that's not a good idea. Your dad doesn't want me to meet them yet." It's a genuine excuse. I want to respect Josh's wishes. But making a good impression on Dan's brothers is the real reason I hesitate. "I'm not good with new people—"

"Screw what my dad wants. And I'll be with you the whole time. Nothing to worry about."

There's something comforting in Dan's words, and even though I'm nervous about meeting his brothers, I can't deny being intrigued by them. "Okay. So, Felix is the oldest, right?"

"Yeah. He's twenty-one." Dan leads the way through the gardens, walking alongside me with his hands in his pockets. "Tyler's a year younger than him, but he's off with his girlfriend tonight. Killian is seventeen."

Dan asks me about my day and how I'm settling into the beach house. I mention liking it here and ask whether he saw the latest photos the paparazzi took of us. I've noticed the cameramen more frequently since that first time my photo was taken on the street. Dan's advice was to ignore the cameras and not search my name on the internet, but I care too much and need to know what's being said about me in the public eye.

A couple of weeks back, a rumor surfaced that I was Dan's girlfriend, all thanks to that first photo where his arm was around my shoulders. I showed him the gossip site, expecting him to be astounded. The only reaction I got out of him was a smirk, like he was pleased by the rumor.

Secretly, I liked his reaction. The girls at school started treating me a little nicer too, thanks to the rumor. When Josh made a public announcement that I'm family and not dating his son, the girls returned to showing no interest in me, as I expected they would.

Within a few minutes, we arrive at the front of the mansion, where a black Chrysler sits in the dark, the only light surrounding us coming from its headlights. I gulp at the sight of two guys dressed in suits, leaning against the car with their arms folded and engaged in a quiet conversation.

I've seen them before in photos, but the photos didn't do justice for how handsome they are. Especially Felix, the oldest one. He's a different kind of handsome to Dan. Not boyish at all. A man, and a dangerous one at that. Slick and sharp and with cunning eyes. Blond hair. The only blond one of the Blackwoods. Tattoos peek above his collar.

Killian has a younger look to him, like Dan. More approachable than Felix, athletic and strong, though he still makes me nervous.

"Hey," Dan announces our arrival.

They both turn to the sound of his voice, their eyes latching onto me, and I feel naked beneath their gazes.

Felix looks at me for five seconds at most before glancing away with a smirk. "Now I see why Dad was hiding you from us."

Killian laughs, nodding at Dan. "Dad is letting *you* near her? He's lost his mind."

"Enough. Don't be dickheads," Dan drones, then lowers his voice to me. "Sorry, I thought they'd behave."

The younger brother continues. "She really is as pretty as you said she is. And she's wearing your hoodie. Cute."

"Killian, shut the fuck up."

He laughs harder. "We're only messing around."

Perhaps I should be more nervous about the downhill direction this meeting is heading in. I now understand why Josh wanted to control my interaction with his sons. But all I can focus on is that Dan told his brothers I'm pretty. And they're implying that, what, Dan might try something on me? A tightness coils in my lower tummy, hot and foreign and... I like this feeling, more than I should.

Finally, it dawns on me that I haven't said a single word to Felix and Killian. I don't know if they're trying to intimidate me or what. If they are, it's working. I need to say something to level the playing field but have no idea how to respond. The longer I contemplate my words, the more I realize I'm standing here like an idiot, so I speak the first thing that comes to mind, pathetic as it may be.

"Thanks. I guess you guys are kind of pretty, too." I try to say the words with bite, but I'm so nervous my voice ends up sounding airy and delicate, like I'm sincerely telling the brothers they're beautiful.

The two of them look at each other, confused and trying to decipher my tone, before Felix cracks a smile at me. "You're a little weird, you know? I like it."

His approval is a shock, yet I'll take it as a win.

"Don't worry, Ally. Whatever our father might think, you're safe around us. After all, we're about to be family."

My brow furrows. "What do you mean?"

"Our father is smitten with Amabella. It's only a matter of time before he proposes."

This is the first time marriage has been brought to my attention. Maybe it's silly of me to have never entertained the idea of Mom and Josh getting married. I hug my body in the cool breeze, processing how the information makes me feel. I like Josh a lot and I'm happy for my mom. Yet, having him as a stepfather would change the dynamics between me and Dan.

I'd no longer have a crush on a random guy, but a crush on my stepbrother. That's weird and wrong and I can only imagine what others would say. It's not like I'll ever act on this crush, but *I* would know the truth, and I wouldn't like it one bit.

"All right, Killian and I are heading back to the city." Felix retrieves car keys from his pocket. "Nice meeting you, baby sis. Dan, keep your dick in your pants."

"Felix, I swear to God," Dan groans. The other two brothers laugh.

I force a smile and say goodbye, barely taking notice of their banter. They drive off, leaving me and Dan alone in the moonlight.

"Sorry, that was kind of intense," Dan says. "Are you okay?"

"Yeah, I'm just stuck on the part about our parents getting married."

I look up at Dan, gauging his reaction to the potential marriage. His eyes are already on me, his jaw stiff. He doesn't say a word, but I sense he's not thrilled about us being step siblings either.

I stare out to the black abyss of the ocean, not truly hearing the waves crash on the shore, not when my mind is a million miles away.

"You're quiet," Dan says, sitting beside me on the sand.

"I'm still thinking about what Felix said about our parents getting married."

"You don't like it?"

"I don't know. I like Josh for my mom. But their marriage would make me your stepsister. I don't like that part."

Dan watches the ocean, not saying a word. He hasn't shared his opinion on the marriage. Perhaps us being step siblings isn't such a big deal for him. He's my only real friend and is quickly becoming the center of my world, but the same can't be said in reverse.

Dan has many friends. He's social and I've seen how everyone flocks to him. Sometimes I catch him looking at me in an intimate way friends don't look at each other. But if I became off limits to him as his stepsister, it wouldn't be such an issue for him, seeing as there's no shortage of girls lining up to be with him.

Yet, still, there are things I wonder about Dan, like has he ever thought about kissing me? Has he ever wanted to have sex with me? I think about those things a lot. Too much, probably.

I don't have the confidence to outright ask him those questions and settle for something a little less obvious. "You told your brothers I'm pretty?"

Dan looks across at me in that familiar way no guy should look at a girl who is just his friend, his gaze on my lips, his voice soft against the crashing waves. "Yeah, I did."

The heat of his eyes warms me. I want him to lean in and kiss me. I don't think I've ever wanted anything as much. Yet, there's something within me that feels ashamed of wanting his kiss. My mom wouldn't approve of my actions, sneaking out and kissing a boy. Not any boy either, but her boyfriend's son. Maybe even fiancé's son, soon.

Dan tears his eyes away from me and peers up at the night sky. "You know you can see Jupiter from this beach."

"Really?"

"Lie back. I'll show you."

I follow Dan's instructions, lying in the sand. He scoots right beside me, making nervous flickers of energy come to life in my chest as he lies back, slipping a hand beneath my shoulders. My breath hitches at the sudden closeness between us as Dan draws me into his chest. The way he's holding me is so innocent yet... it doesn't feel innocent at all.

We've touched before, with brief hugs or when I'm giving piano lessons and correcting his hands, but never has he held me like this. I don't know much about guys, but this *has* to be more than friendship.

"You see that star there?" Dan points, his words a deep murmur against my temple.

I'm too consumed by his scent and the warmth of being in his arms to pay attention to the stars, and nod on autopi-lot. My eyelids fall shut and my breathing gradually slows in time with Dan's. The waves continue rolling onto the shore, the white noise lulling me into a deep relaxation.

"Are you tired?" he whispers, breaking the silence.

"Yes, but I don't want to leave. I could sleep just like this."

"Then sleep." Dan pulls me closer and strokes my hair as I drift to sleep. The last thing I remember is a kiss on my forehead and Dan murmuring, "I think you're the most beautiful girl I've ever seen, Ally."

Chapter 5

Dan

Three months later, Saturday, September 1

SHARING A BED WITH MY... SHE'S NOT MY STEPSISTER YET

My father raises his champagne glass at the end of his speech. "To Amabella, our children, and this beautiful family union we're about to form."

A sea of hands lifts their glasses. Here we are, the end of summer, back in the city to celebrate my father and Amabella's engagement, right before my junior year of high school starts. The penthouse is filled with their closest friends and family. Thousands of dollars have been thrown into this party, with the finest catering and decorations. The press is even here, with journalists and photographers reporting on the hottest new couple in New York City.

The media says Amabella Hastings has turned bachelor Josh Blackwood into a changed man, leaving his hotel empire behind, the two of them now delving into their passion for philanthropy. She's left her seating hostess job. Together, Dad and Amabella have founded a nonprofit called Forever Families.

The organization's mission is to support and strengthen families in need with whatever help they require—domestic violence counseling, adoption, medical treatment, the list goes on. It's an admirable venture, yet it pisses me off that my father is suddenly all about supporting other families when he's been the most absent father my entire life.

What pisses me off more is that the Blackwoods are now the public face of Forever Families. We're meant to be showcasing how strong and united our blended family is. It's the biggest fucking joke I've ever heard. I'm expected to act like the perfect son and role model citizen, when I was never consulted about any of this. On top of all that, I spend most of my time with the biggest hard-on for Ally. Real great family we've got here.

"Let's get a family photo," a journalist calls out.

Biting down my distaste, I step up to Dad and Amabella, where Killian already has his arm around Amabella's shoulders, the two of them laughing over something. Tyler stands alongside them with his girlfriend Harper, and Felix is saying something quiet to Dad. Ally joins last of all with a timid smile on her face, hating the public spotlight. She tacks onto the opposite side of the group from me, hiding herself behind Felix.

"Baby sis, you belong right in the middle." Felix jabs her ribs. She jerks away from him, squealing and laughing, but he hooks an arm around her shoulders and pulls her in close. She caves and hugs Felix around the waist, smiling at the cameras and truly looking happy.

My brothers have all taken a strong liking toward Ally, in an innocent, brotherly way, as I should have. They like

Amabella, too. The two girls are pretty much the only reason any of us can tolerate being around my father. None of us have a good relationship with him, but mine is the most damaged. I feel his judgment more than my brothers do, and I know it's because of my mother's death.

The marriage proposal happened in The Hamptons, and when we returned to the city a week ago, Amabella and Ally moved into the penthouse with us. It's both the best and worst thing that's ever happened to me.

Now, I have Ally with me constantly, sleeping in the bedroom next to mine. She's already transformed the room into her own little sanctuary. I spend most of my time in there with her, watching her play the piano, taking piano lessons from her, laughing, talking. My God, she can talk, and about the most random shit. She's not shy at all around me anymore and I love it.

Dad had quiet words with me and Killian, about how we now have two women living with us and need to act respectable by not bringing girls home. I wouldn't want Ally to see me with another girl anyway. Now, I go to the girl's home whenever I... need to get Ally out of my system.

It's wrong. I shouldn't think about Ally when I'm with another girl, but I do. She's *all* I can think about. On the days I don't have sex, I jerk off to the thought of Ally, how innocent she is and how I want to be the one to corrupt her.

As soon as our family photo has been taken, I make my escape out to the balcony with a glass of whiskey everyone assumes is cola, wanting to avoid any journalists. I rest my forearms on the railing, gazing out at the surrounding buildings all lit up in the night. Guests are mingling, but thankfully none of them seek me out.

"Thank you, son." My shoulders clench at the sound of my father's voice behind me. I don't look his way as he joins me at the railing. "I want you to know how much I appreciate your acceptance of Amabella and Ally into this family, and how you've befriended Ally. I really hope we can all be a strong family together."

For fuck's sake. He's been absent my entire life, and *now* he wants to be a family? I intend to treat Amabella as family. But my dad can get fucked.

I sip my drink, turning away from my father and dismissing him with my back.

"What car do you have your eye on?"

I glance over my shoulder at him. "What are you talking about?"

"I told you I'd buy you a car if you cooperated with me."

Right, the car. I'd forgotten all about that arrangement since the first moment I saw Ally. I could play along, pretending the car is the whole reason I've put so much effort into getting to know Ally and her mother. Maybe it's the safest bet, to ensure my father doesn't catch on to how much I want to fuck Ally.

But cashing in on this deal feels wrong when Ally means far more to me than a car. I'm attached to her, more than I thought possible. The first time I saw her, I was admittedly taken by her looks. Yes, my thoughts are in the gutter about her every day, and she's nothing like the crowd I normally hang around, but her personality is so precious and funny. She's talented and genuine, an all-round good person, and I find myself wanting to spend all my time with her.

Ally tells me I make her feel safe. Hearing those words brings a warmth to my chest I've never felt before. I don't know what that warmth means, but I like that I'm such a comfort to her. I *will* keep her safe and always protect her. Somehow, in a matter of months, she's become my closest friend. And I do *not* have friends who are girls.

I can't deny I want to fuck Ally. I'm sure Ally knows it, too. It'll never happen, though. She's off limits now that Dad and Amabella are getting married. I hate it, but getting to know Amabella over the summer has made me realize there's more than just my happiness at stake here.

For the first time in my life, it feels like I have a mother. Amabella spends time talking to me each day, *really* talking and listening, learning about my life. She asks about school and what interests I have. She even took me to high tea one day, just the two of us. It was weird but also one of the best outings I've had.

On that day, she opened up about her ex-boyfriend and the disgusting ways he treated her, how he was so aggressive that she had to be admitted to the hospital, and the guilt she feels for exposing Ally to that behavior. She told me it's been terrible to watch Ally struggle with confidence and friendships but how grateful she is that Ally and I have become such close friends.

After all the shit Amabella has gone through in her past, she deserves the happiness she's finally found with my father, and I'm not going to fuck it up by coming between them just because I want to sleep with Ally.

"I don't want a car." I shoot the rest of my drink down and face my father. "Ally and Amabella mean a lot to me. Put the money toward buying Ally a grand piano and jewelry for Amabella. A welcome to the family gesture."

He's dumbfounded for a moment, probably wondering if I'm fucking with him—that *is* something I would do—until he sees the serious expression on my face. He nods with approval, smiling at me for the first time in I can't remember how long.

"That's a thoughtful gesture. I'm proud of you, son."

I scoff and turn back to the railing. The one time he's ever been proud of me.

As soon as Dad returns inside, Felix steps beside me, amusement slick on his face. "Dad bribed you?"

"He asked me to behave around Amabella and Ally."

"You've behaved around Amabella. Ally..." He smirks. "I'm not so sure."

I send him a foul look. "It's not like that. We're friends and about to be family."

"If you say so." He places his drink on the railing and pats my shoulder. "We've made enough of an appearance tonight. What do you say we ditch the party for a game of poker."

The engagement party continues in the living room while me, Felix, and Killian crowd around a table in my bedroom with a bunch of cards and poker chip towers scattered across the table. The room is dark, with only a neon lamp on my bedside table, casting a red glow.

As we play and sip on whiskey, Felix tells us about a new business venture of his, seeing as he's just come of age and received the last installment of his trust fund. We all laugh as he tells us how proud Dad is of him, becoming a business owner and opening a cocktail lounge. What Dad doesn't know, and what Felix tells us in confidence, is that the real business will be an illegal speakeasy hidden beneath the cocktail lounge.

A knock on my bedroom door interrupts the conversation. "Yeah?" I call out.

The door opens and Ally's head peeks inside. Fuck,

she's pretty tonight with a pink, frilly dress, ballet flats, and that satin ribbon she always has in her hair. She looks like a doll, and I have to be careful not to stare. All I can think about is undressing her. Wrapping her legs around my waist. Feeling how tight she'd be.

"Just in time." Felix pulls up a fourth chair. "We're about to start a new game. Sit."

"You know I'll lose again." Ally steps into the red room anyway, joining us with a smile. She likes being a part of this.

The three of us have insisted on teaching Ally poker, telling her it's an initiation into the family. The parents disapproved when they found out, saying she's too young to gamble. I could see Ally wanted to talk back, pointing out that me and Killian aren't of legal age to gamble either. But Ally, always the good little girl she is, never says anything out of line.

So, we teach Ally the game in secret. There's no harm done; she's so bad at poker that we never make her bet any money. It's just a bit of fun and sibling bonding, as I told Dad and Amabella that first night they found us. That occasion made me feel real dirty when I referred to Ally as my sister. Right before, I'd jerked off to the thought of her lips wrapped tight around my cock.

"I heard laughing before I entered the room," Ally says, peeking at her cards once Felix has dealt our hand. Her lips twitch with excitement. I smother a laugh; she has the worst poker face I've ever encountered. "What were you all laughing over?"

Felix winks at her. "Just some shit with Dad. Can't tell you."

She looks at the three of us. "No Tyler again? What's the deal with him never being around?"

It's subtle but I don't miss the way Felix tenses at her question. "The short version: we don't get along."

Killian laughs. "Dan and I get along with Tyler."

"What's the long version?" Ally asks.

"We're still trying to figure that one out," I tell her, and it's the truth.

I have no clue what shit has gone down between Felix and Tyler. They were somewhat close growing up, being practically the same age. In Felix's last year of high school, Dad sent him across the country to finish his education with boarding school.

When he returned, Felix and Tyler weren't on speaking terms. Neither of them will tell us why. Since the rift started between them, Tyler has become distant from everyone in the family. He's the brother I have the least connection with.

Ally takes the hint, along with me and Killian, to drop the questioning. We play a game of poker, sharing a few laughs and stories with each other. Ally loses, of course. When midnight arrives, the engagement party starts to wrap up and we call it a night. Felix heads home. Killian returns to his bedroom. Ally helps me pack away the poker chips and cards.

"I guess I should take a shower and go to bed," she says, heading for the adjoining bathroom that connects our two bedrooms.

I always thought sharing a bathroom with a girl would be annoying. That their belongings would take over my space. Well, they do, but it's not even the least bit annoying. Ally has perfume bottles and skin care products spread across the counter. I like how she's made herself at home, and how everywhere I look, something reminds me of her.

"I'm not tired," I say, right before she enters the bathroom. I've been thinking about getting her alone all night, and now's my chance. "You want to stay and watch a movie or something?"

She shrugs. "Sure."

I slip out of my shoes and suit jacket and loosen the buttons at my collar to be more comfortable. Grabbing my laptop, I log into Netflix, then turn off my red neon light, switching to a more relaxing neon blue lamp instead.

"What's with the neon lights?" Ally asks while I sit in bed, beneath the covers, scrolling for something to watch.

I look up from the screen, finding her standing at the foot of my bed. "What do you mean?"

"I've been living here a week and not once have I seen your bedroom under normal light. You have about five different neon lamps and one of them is always on."

"I have an affinity with neon lights and how they make me feel."

"And how's that?" she asks.

"Relaxed. They remind me of gambling dens. I like the darkness that comes with them. The silhouettes. You also look very pretty in neon lighting."

Ally meets my gaze, not saying anything, but this girl always says so much with her eyes. She likes that I'm attracted to her. She wants to be kissed. *More* than kissed. She thinks about sex a lot.

"You gonna watch the movie standing up?" I ask when Ally remains at the foot of my bed.

She bites her bottom lip. "Where am I supposed to sit?"

"In bed with me."

"Is that... okay?" Her voice turns thin. She's suddenly nervous around me, which is kind of cute.

"Get in the fucking bed, Ally. We're just watching a movie."

She laughs and steps out of her ballet flats before climbing in, beneath the covers too, *right* beside me. This is what it's been like between us ever since that night she fell asleep in my arms on the beach. When we're alone, we sit closer to each other than we should. Sometimes I'll hold her hand. We'll watch movies on the couch with my arm draped around her shoulders.

Only *ever* when we're alone.

And *never* do we talk about it, both of us knowing the way we act is wrong.

This is the first time she's entered my bed. I shouldn't have suggested it. This is definitely crossing the line. But now that she's here, so close to me, I can't resist and slip my arm around her waist, pulling her even closer, till she's all but sitting in my lap.

This close up, even with the neon blue light, I can see Ally blushing. She won't meet my eyes, and looks straight at the laptop screen, but I see the slightest traces of a smile on her lips. She likes this. Maybe as much as I do. I'm trying, most definitely failing, at stopping myself from getting hard.

She's not my girlfriend, but in moments like this, it feels like she is.

I live for moments like this.

We watch the movie in silence, occasionally making comments and laughing with each other. By two in the morning, when the closing credits rise up the screen and it's time for Ally to return to her bedroom, she snuggles into me.

"Can I sleep in here tonight?"

Fuck. Yes. *Please.*

I shut the laptop and place it onto my bedside table, along with switching the neon light off, leaving us in darkness. My arms slide around Ally as I pull her into a hug beneath the covers, her back flush to my chest, my lips on the nape of her neck, and with my hand pressed to her lower stomach. Dad and Amabella would freak out if they found us in bed like this, but what they don't know won't hurt them.

I feel Ally's breath accelerate. Her heart is pounding as fast as mine. Though I've been in bed with a lot of girls, this is all new for me. I've never actually slept next to a girl or even cuddled. I could get used to this with Ally.

"Your dress is ridiculous," I murmur, the fabric all bunched up and bulky beneath my hand.

"You don't like it?"

"I love it. I love everything you wear. I was referring to your dress being ridiculous sleepwear." I think back to how much I liked Ally wearing my hoodie that first night at the beach house. "You want to wear one of my shirts instead?"

She hesitates before answering with a nod.

Using my phone flashlight, I grab a shirt from my drawer and pass it to Ally. Once the flashlight is off and I'm back in bed, Ally changes into my shirt and returns to my arms. Fucking perfection.

"You love everything I wear?" she asks quietly.

"Yeah. I love your style. Cute and innocent, much like you as a person."

Her breath shudders. She's so warm in my arms. "I don't feel very innocent right now. But technically we're not doing anything wrong, just hugging in bed. Friends can hug."

"Right." She's not my stepsister yet. That's what I tell myself.

This thing between us is intimate but completely inno- cent, and that's the way it has to stay because I can't fuck Ally, no matter how bad I want to.

Chapter 6

Dan

Six weeks later, Wednesday, October 15

THE NEON CARDS

One minute past midnight. It's not my birthday anymore.
Thank fuck.

I arrive home, drunk, in a terrible mood, and with the
brunette who insisted she come home with me to make me
feel better. Ally is spending the night at her uncle Daxton's
apartment, otherwise there's no way I would have invited
the brunette back here. We met at a random party tonight.
She tells me her name is Tiffany.

She clutches my hand with reservation as soon as we
step through the front door. "The lights are on. I thought
you said everyone would be asleep."

"They are asleep."

Amabella probably left the lights on for me. She does
motherly things like that. Any other day of the year I'd

appreciate her maternal ways. Right now, it's a reminder of how I've never known my own mother.

For the past couple of years, I've spent each birthday drunk and away from my family because it's easier this way, to block out that my mother died giving birth to me and how my father never formed a bond with me because of it. I've never stopped feeling guilty over my brothers growing up without their mother. I'd rather not spend the day pretending to be happy. Most of all, I can't deal with my father acting as though we have any kind of relationship.

He and my brothers know to give me space on this day. Ally and Amabella are new to the scene and insisted on celebrating my birthday. It took some convincing for them to agree that I be left alone.

The alcohol's buzz is wearing off. I need a distraction from the weight of my birthday and how every day, all day, all I can think about is undressing Ally and kissing every part of her body. She recently told me she's a virgin. I'd already guessed as much, but hearing the words made me that much more desperate to take her first time and teach her how to ride my cock.

Just thinking about that visual has me hard right now. The brunette notices and smiles. It's a sloppy smile, impacted by the alcohol. But she's only drunk enough to be tipsy, so I don't feel bad leading her to my bedroom. I need to fuck something hard and come to the thought of my pretty blond.

As soon as I've closed my bedroom door behind us, Tiffany is tugging off my jacket and shirt. She strips out of her dress, completely naked but for a thong.

Someone knocks on the door. "I'm busy," I call, staring at the tits in front of me.

"Dan?"

Fuck.

I'm instantly sober at the sound of Ally's voice. She calls out my name, filled with concern. Panic rushes through me at the thought of her finding me in here with another girl. What the fuck is she doing home?

"Who's that?" Tiffany asks, loud enough for Ally to hear, and I quickly place a hand over her mouth.

"I can't talk right now," I call out to Ally.

"Yeah, I can tell." Her voice flips to pure sarcasm. The tone is sharp, unlike anything I've ever heard from Ally. "I sent you a text earlier, asking if you were okay. Would have been nice if you replied."

I groan with frustration and open the door halfway, hiding Tiffany behind it. Ally stands before me, wrapped in a pink dressing gown. Her eyes drop to my bare torso and her cheeks flash red. A second later, she looks at something on the floor behind me, and I realize it's Tiffany's dress.

I kick the dress out of view. "I thought you were at Daxton's house tonight. I wouldn't have brought—"

She scoffs. "Please, Dan, you're allowed to fuck whoever you want, and clearly you do."

I suck in a surprised breath. This is the first time I've heard Ally swear and it sounds so vulgar coming from her mouth. She knows I have sex with girls. We don't talk about it with each other, but she knows. She's been aware from the very start. The only thing she doesn't know is that sleeping with girls is my way of keeping her at bay, redirecting the sexual frustration I have over her, because if I don't have a sexual outlet, I'll end up losing control and fucking her.

And that *can't* happen.

Regardless, Ally seeing me with a girl right in front of her face is more confronting than just being aware of my habits, and I can't blame her for being mad. She sneaks into my bed most nights, ever since the engagement party a few weeks back. Though all we do is sleep tangled in each other's arms, and though there's no commitment between us, those sleepovers are intimate. Sleeping in someone's arms has an intimacy that even sex can't offer.

"I asked for privacy today," I tell her. When I saw her text come through, it made me feel like even more of a fuck up, knowing the feelings for her that I shouldn't have. With all the weight attached to my birthday, I didn't want to face my feelings for Ally.

She glares at me. "I gave you privacy. But a simple text to let me know you were okay would have been nice. You tell me your birthday is the worst day of your year, how can I not worry about you?" Ally reaches into the pocket of her dressing gown and retrieves a small package, shoving it against my chest. "Here. I got you a present."

"I asked you not to do that."

"I know. I guess I'm an idiot and decided I care about you too much to listen. It won't happen again."

She enters her bedroom and slams the door, the lock clicking shut. I rake a hand through my hair and swear. Upsetting Ally is the last thing I want to do. Maybe I was too harsh on her.

I knock on her bedroom door and call out her name. When there's no answer, I look down at the present in my hand and unwrap it. Inside is a deck of playing cards. I pull them out of their package and skim through them, each one black and with neon skull artwork. I rest my forehead against her door and groan, feeling more guilty. Ally gave me the perfect present—personal, simple—and here I am being a dick to her.

I hate that I've upset her, this girl who, with just one

look, one smile, makes me feel like the center of the universe. She doesn't have many trusted people in her life, which makes being one of her trusted people feel so much more special and rewarding. It's sad that so few people get to see the side of her that I do. The fun, dedicated, caring girl.

"Ally." I knock on her door again, my voice quiet. "I'm sorry. Please let me in. I love the present."

No answer. I return to my bedroom and enter our shared bathroom, trying the door handle to her room, finding it locked too.

"Dan," the naked girl in my bed calls. "Are you coming?"

I return to my room and hand the girl her dress. "You need to leave."

Chapter 7

Ally

The same day, Wednesday, October 15

"You're my person"

I leave school after my last class for the day. Like clockwork, Dan is leaning against the gate, waiting for me. Only this time, he has a bouquet of red roses in his hands. He catches sight of me and presses off the gate, approaching with an apology in his eyes.

We haven't spoken since last night when he came home drunk and with a girl. He normally walks me to school, but I left before he woke this morning. I didn't know what to say to Dan, that I hated how he brought a girl home? I did, and he knows it. But regardless of the closeness we've developed, it's unreasonable to expect he doesn't sleep with other girls. I'm not his girlfriend. Our parents will be married within a few months, for God's sake.

The girl isn't the main issue.

I pass through the school gates without saying a word to Dan. "Ally," he calls, his footsteps speeding up to catch me.

I walk faster, weaving through the after-school crowd of girls exiting the campus. Dan keeps calling my name, his voice growing closer. When I'm free from the herd of students, my speed increases, but it doesn't take long for Dan to match my stride.

"I'm sorry about last night, Ally. I asked the girl to leave immediately."

"I'm the one who's sorry." I keep walking. "I got my feelings hurt by caring too much about you. You told me to give you space on your birthday. I should have listened."

"That doesn't excuse me being a dick. I should have replied to your message. Ally, I love the cards you bought me." Dan steps in front of me, blocking my path and bringing us face to face. Finally, I'm forced to stop and look up at him, at the sincerity in his eyes and the bouquet he holds out for me. "I'm sorry about the girl," he repeats himself in a gentle tone. "I'm sorry about everything. You have to forgive me because you're my person and I don't know what I'll do if you stay angry at me."

My heart skips a beat. "Your person?"

"My favorite person. My..." He groans and speaks in a softer, more intimate tone. "This thing between us... It's so complicated. I wish you were my girlfr—"

"Don't say the word." My blood vibrates with heat over Dan's confession. Hearing that word almost leave his mouth. The thought of being Dan's girlfriend... that he *wants* me to be his girlfriend... It's wrong yet so goddamn tempting that it hurts. "We both know *that* can't happen."

My gosh, I can't even bring myself to say *girlfriend* out loud, not when referring to me and Dan. Whenever we touch or hug or do anything intimate, it's never verbally acknowledged between us. If we don't acknowledge it, somehow, the behavior feels more acceptable.

I often wonder what would happen if I did push for us to be together. The reality of us together would be awkward and socially unacceptable. Even if others did accept us, what if we broke up? That would be more awkward, being forced to see each other all the time. Plus, I'd lose the only real friend I have.

On top of all those issues, there's the ramifications our relationship would have in the public eye. It wouldn't be a good image for Forever Families, scandalous even, when our family is the face of a charity in support of helping families.

"I know it can't happen," he says.

"Which is why you should continue seeing that girl from last night." The words are a struggle to get out, hating the thought of Dan having sex with girls. But I mean what I say. If he's out there sleeping around, it makes this easier for me, knowing he's not mine. "You should date other girls too. Or just sleep with them. Whatever it is you do—"

"Ally." My name on his lips is a gentle hush. "I'm sorry. There are things I wish I could say to you. I would say them if our parents weren't..." He cuts himself off. His gaze bores through me with such sincerity.

I sigh, knowing I can't stay mad at him, not when he looks at me like this and talks in such a way. Our situation is complicated, as he said, and neither of us know how to handle these feelings.

"You don't have to say any of those things. I think I understand." The tension releases from my shoulders and I accept the bouquet with a soft smile. "You're my person too. You're the first person to have ever bought me flowers. I love them. Thank you."

"You're the only girl I've ever bought them for." He

grins, and I'm melting over how tender his eyes are upon me. Dan digs a hand into his pocket, pulling out his phone. "I'd like to show you something."

He taps a few times on the screen then turns it in my direction, displaying an old photograph of a pregnant woman with three young boys at her side. I recognize Dan's eyes in her instantly, and my chest warms. Tears prick in my eyes, not because I'm sad for Dan but because he's sharing something so guarded with me and how special it feels for him to let me in like this.

"This is your mother? Dan, she's beautiful."

"I feel a lot of guilt over her death and what it's done to my family. I don't want to shut you out, though. I know a lot of girls, Ally. You're the only one that matters to me."

I smile, blinking away the tears. "Thank you for showing me the photo. It means a lot to me."

In the back of my mind, a warning signal goes off, that I'm getting in too deep with my feelings for Dan. I should stop sleeping in his bed but I know I won't. And the flower gesture, though an apology, feels romantic and inappropriate, like what a guy *would* buy for his girlfriend.

Perhaps the roses sum up our dynamics perfectly because there's nothing appropriate about the way Dan called me his person.

He drapes an arm over my shoulders and we walk side by side all the way home from school. There's nothing appropriate about that either. But just like every other time I hear that warning signal, I push it away, because being Dan's person is intoxicating and addictive.

The Second Year

Temptation

Chapter 8

Dan

Another summer at our beach house comes to an end, this time spent as an official family. Six months Dad and Amabella have been married.

I'm now a guy who drools over his stepsister, who steals glances at her every chance I can get. Her pretty lips. Her perfect ass. The incredible tits she's recently grown.

Ally will be a junior in high school as of next week, me a senior, and she's looking more developed with each passing day. More ready for sex, though that shouldn't be a thought that crosses my mind. She's started dressing in more revealing clothes. Classy, of course; everything about Ally is elegant, and still with the lace, bows, and frills. But her necklines have grown a little deeper and her dresses a little shorter.

It's evening and I'm playing a piano duet with Ally in

the living room of the beach house, both of us laughing as our fingers brush against each other's, battling it out to press certain keys. She reaches across me to play her notes, her breasts grazing against my arm. Half the time, I wonder if this is why she teaches me duets, so we can get close and touch each other.

From my peripheral, someone enters the living room, joining us by the piano. Ally and I stop playing, looking up at the same time to find Killian.

He rests a forearm on the piano top. "Carlie Montgomery is throwing a party tonight at her parents' beach house. You two interested in attending?"

I'm pretty sure Killian is fucking Carlie. The Montgomerys are family friends, their beach house not too far from here. When Killian isn't off with Carlie, he's been hanging out with me and Ally a lot this summer—Felix too, when he visits—the four of us entertaining ourselves with the pool, the tennis courts, the beach, even chasing each other through the hedge maze. We play poker, which Ally is still terrible at. She insists I keep teaching her how to improve, that poker is an interest of mine and she wants to get good at it for me.

I'm surprised Killian is still inviting Ally to these parties. There have been a few spread throughout the summer I've attended with him. Ally always chooses to stay back with Dad and Amabella, saying it's not her scene. I know it's because she's had bad experiences with people at school. I've asked her to come along with me, feeling bad for leaving her behind, but she always turns down the offer.

"I'll stay home from the party with Ally," I say.

"Who's to say Ally is staying home?" Killian grins. "Ally, you keen?"

"You know these parties aren't her scene." I give the

response a little too fast and a little too sharp, and Ally frowns at me.

The amount of male attention she'd receive at these parties would be tough for me to stomach. We've already discussed how we can't be together, but from the way we act in private, it feels like Ally is my girl.

Back in the city, with our connected bedrooms, she's continued climbing into my bed most nights, teasing me by wearing short pajama pants that barely cover her ass. I always pull her to my chest, holding her close with one hand on her lower stomach beneath her shirt, flush against her skin.

I can't count the number of times I've wanted to slip my hand beneath her panties and feel how wet she is, then push my fingers inside her pussy and make her come. I know she's felt my dick hard against her back many times. I know she likes it from the way she presses back against it.

Our parents are under the impression we formed such a strong friendship as a result of Ally not having friends, and that we truly are just friends. I mean, it's not a total lie. My brothers believe it too. There were a few comments from Killian and Felix back when Ally and I first met, implying that perhaps something more was happening between us, but I convinced them otherwise. I can't risk anyone finding out about me and Ally. The little intimacy I do get with her would instantly be over.

"You don't want me at the party?" she asks me.

"I didn't say that. You've never shown an interest before. I didn't want you to feel like Killian was forcing you into anything."

She presses her lips together, deep in thought. "I know I'm not the best around new people. Are you embarrassed to be seen with me?"

"Of course not." And it's the goddamn truth.

"Well, what will it be?" Killian prompts. "Could be fun. Your first party. I'll get you drunk."

"Killian," I snap, glaring at him. "She's never had a drop of alcohol in her life. She's not getting drunk."

"I'll go," Ally says. "I won't drink, but I'd like to see what's so fun about these parties."

"Great. We'll leave in an hour," Killian says, exiting the living room.

Ally makes a move to follow him, but I grab her wrist before she can stand from the piano stool. "You don't have to go to this party if you don't want to. I'll stay back with you."

"I want to go. Mom and Josh said I can attend these parties as long as I have you and Killian looking out for me."

"Because they don't know what goes down at these parties."

She retrieves her wrist from me and laughs, the sound purposefully sweet, like she's playing up her innocence. "And what does go down at these parties that you can't bear me to be around? Drinking? Drugs? Sex? Maybe I *want* to have sex."

"Ally..."

"*You* don't want me having sex. Is that it?"

She holds my gaze, the two of us staring at each other in silence, but I know she can read my annoyance of her question.

"Yes," I finally say. "I don't want you having sex with a random guy at a party."

She rolls her eyes, with that sweet little laugh again, and stands from the piano stool. "I need to get dressed."

I watch her leave, swearing under my breath. I almost run after Ally, desperate to make her promise she'll stay by my side tonight and not hook up with any guys. But she has every right to be with another guy. I'm not creating double standards here, and I can't keep pretending like she's mine. Sooner or later, she'll find a boyfriend and I'll need to learn to be okay with it.

Returning to my own room, I take a shower and get dressed into jeans and a hoodie, dreading this upcoming party. I wait for Ally and Killian by the front door, shuffling the neon deck of cards Ally bought me for my birthday, trying to calm myself. I carry the deck around with me everywhere. It feels like holding onto a piece of Ally, even when others are around. Whenever I'm stressed or frustrated after having an argument with my father, I shuffle the cards, thinking about Ally, and it calms me. It's my most cherished possession.

Tonight, the cards do nothing to help soothe me. This party feels like the beginning of the end between me and Ally. She'll find a guy she's interested in. The only reason she hasn't already found someone is because of that all-girls school she attends, and how she doesn't socialize outside of school. There'll be no more secret sleepovers where she sneaks into my bed. She won't let me hold her when we're in private.

A door upstairs opens, I hear footsteps, then Ally appears, descending the stairs. Blood rushes to my cock at the sight of her. My muscles clench and I realize I'm grinding my molars. She's wearing a strapless white beach dress that hugs her tits in the most incredible way. The bottom is flowy and skims the floor, with a slit all the way to the top of her thigh.

"What the fuck are you wearing?" I glare at her. "Go back upstairs and get changed."

She looks down at herself and shrugs. "What's wrong

with this? Killian said beach party. I've been wearing this dress all summer and you've never had an issue with it."

"Every guy at the party will be hitting on you and trying to get into your pants, then later jerking off to the thought of you."

Her lips twitch like she's pleased by my response. I've never used such vulgar language around her, and I don't think she's opposed to it. "And that's a problem, why?"

"Ally..."

Killian calls out to us from upstairs, asking if we're ready to leave.

Before he joins us, Ally steps up to me, gazing into my eyes in a playfully innocent way that makes me forget my own name. The tiniest smile dances on her lips as she whispers, "I know you're only trying to be a protective older brother, but I can handle myself. And besides, I wore this dress because I thought *you* might like it." She walks by me, opening the front door and peeking back at me. "I only ever wear things I think you'll like."

Fuck.

My dick throbs, hearing her speak in such subtle ways that say so much. I hate that she's my stepsister. So then why am I turned on by Ally referring to me as her big brother? We've been trying to ignore how we're now family. It's so unexpected that this innocent girl would be the one to mention our new sibling dynamic and make it sexual. Deep down, she really can't be that innocent if this is her way of flirting with me. Having this new piece of knowledge about Ally makes me even more feral for her.

I follow Ally out to the front porch, the two of us alone for a moment, but not for long when I hear Killian's footsteps down the staircase.

Taking my chance, I step up behind Ally, my hand on

her stomach, and press her against my hard cock. A little gasp escapes her as I whisper in her ear. "I love your tits in that dress. You don't leave my side tonight. Understand?"

She nods, and we instantly step away from each other before Killian sees us.

Chapter 9

Ally

The same evening, Saturday, August 20
Queen of Hearts

For a moment there, back on the porch of our beach house, Dan made me feel like his girlfriend when he pressed me against his dick and told me to stay by his side at the party. I loved the way he looked at me in my dress, like I was his, and how he wanted me to feel the effect I have on his body. I agreed to his words because being with Dan was the only place I wanted to be.

Now that we're at the party, staying by Dan's side is turning out to be my idea of hell.

It's an emphasis on what I already knew but had been ignoring—that he acts differently around me. Everyone is throwing alcohol his way, questioning why he's not drinking tonight or being the life of the party. Guys have started talking about "pussy" with Dan, being crude, and only shutting up when noticing me standing quietly beside him.

So many girls have run up and hugged Dan, blatantly flirting and sending him fuck-me eyes. He politely shuts them down, but if I weren't here, I know he'd be into them. He'd take one of them to a bedroom upstairs where they'd have sex, and I'd have no right to be jealous because I've told him there's no *us*.

The worst part about being here with Dan is when he introduces me to the girls, trying to involve me in conversation. The girls barely acknowledge me before they're flirting with Dan again. It reminds me of the girls at school and how they don't talk to me. How I have no friends.

Dan probably doesn't want to be talking to me either right now. His social life is separated into two fragments— me and everyone else—and is intersecting right now, messing everything up for him. I'm interfering with his chances to party with his friends and hook up with girls.

To make matters worse, the music is too loud. I can feel its heavy bass pulsing through my entire body, and it makes me nauseous. There were too many people crowding the inside of the house, but even out here by the pool is no better. There are people all around us, drunk and bumping into me. Guys are shouting, being boisterous with their friends, cannonballing into the pool and splashing me.

A group of girls are talking to Dan by the pool's edge, all wearing bikinis that barely cover their ass and breasts. I'm standing beside him not knowing what to say, looking like a loser. When I find a break in conversation, I take a chance, complimenting one of the girls on her hair, but another guy jumps into the pool and my voice isn't heard.

The conversation continues and I feel like an idiot, growing bright red with embarrassment. I realize my teeth are grinding together and that I'm clutching my elbows.

Every muscle in my body is tense and my breathing is growing more shallow by the second.

This is how it always starts.

My heart pumps faster, knowing what's about to happen, and that I stupidly left my medication at the beach house. My God, I can't have a panic attack at this party and not in front of Dan. He's never witnessed one of my episodes before, and the thought of him seeing me like this is mortifying. It's worse than him seeing how awkward I am around all these new people.

I reach up on my toes, shouting into Dan's ear to be heard over the music, giving him the first excuse for escape I can think of. "I'm going to find Killian."

I manage one step away from Dan before his arm slinks around my waist and he pulls me back to his side. "Killian is probably off with a girl. Stay here." His arm drops from my side, and he speaks to the girls again. "Ally is an incredible musician."

His conversation starter only heightens my discomfort. Dan is trying to include me, and it makes me feel even more pathetic that he has to handhold me in social situations. The girls look at me with disinterest. Clearly none of them want to be talking about me or to me. They only do it to please Dan.

"What kind of musician?" a redhead asks me, her voice bland and not carrying any of the enthusiasm it possessed a moment ago when flirting with Dan.

"Piano," I answer, barely loud enough.

I should say something else. A normal person would elaborate and lead this conversation into something deeper. But I can't speak, no matter how hard I try to force myself. My mind is a clutter of panic and embarrassment. My throat clenches and heat prickles in my eyes like I'm about to cry. What the hell is wrong with me? I *cannot* be about to cry, and the fact that I am only makes everything worse. Can they all tell there are tears in my eyes? They must think I'm weird. Which, I am. This inability to socialize is not normal.

"I need to use the bathroom," I blurt out, seeking another escape.

"I'll take you," Dan says.

"No, it's fine. I'll be back in a second."

"I don't want you going off on your own. It could be hard to find each other again."

The redhead winks at him. "I'll take her. I need to go too. Stay and chat with everyone."

I don't know if the girl thinks she's doing her friends a favor, taking one for the team by getting me away from Dan, but I'll go along with her plan if it means Dan doesn't see me break down.

"Thanks, but I'll take Ally," Dan insists.

My God, he won't give up. Needing to get away from him, I find it within me to smile and laugh at him. "Seriously, have fun with your friends. I'll be right back."

Dan watches me with concern, his brows drawn together, but I guess my laugh was convincing enough because he doesn't follow me and the redhead through the crowd.

As soon as I break free from Dan, my resolve crumbles and tears stream down my cheeks as I follow the girl into the house. She doesn't notice me crying. She's talking about something, but I can't hear anything other than the thumping of my pulse in my ears and the loud music. I'm burning up and need to get somewhere private where no one can see me.

We climb a flight of stairs, arriving at a corridor with

fewer people in sight. "The line for this bathroom should be much shorter than the one downstairs," the girl says to me.

I wipe my face dry before she turns around and sees me crying, but I know I've failed to hide my emotions when she stares at my eyes.

"Shit. Are you okay?" she asks.

"Um, yeah." My chin trembles with my answer. Panicking, I spot an empty bedroom nearby and rush inside, locking the door behind me. It's dark in here and I'm in such a flustered state that I can't find the light switch. But being alone is all that matters.

The girl calls out from the other side of the door, trying the handle. "Hey, let me in."

"I'm fine. I just want a moment to be alone."

She doesn't say anything else. Her shadow disappears from beneath the doorway, and I collapse onto the edge of the bed, bracing my head between my knees and crying uncontrollably.

I don't know how much time passes, all that registers is panic, that I'm trapped at this party. I can't call my parents for help. Mom would freak out, that the one time she let me attend a party, placing trust in Dan and Killian to look out for me, I wind up having a panic attack. The boys would no doubt get a stern speaking to from Josh, when none of this is their fault.

I can't call for Dan. I'll die if he sees me like this. We've known each other for a little over a year now, and while I've been honest about my difficulties in new social situations, he's never witnessed one of my panic attacks. He thinks I'm this amazing girl, and I can't bear the thought of that changing.

Killian is my only option for help, if he answers his

phone. He's probably off with a girl, like Dan said, and will be too distracted to take my call.

"She went in there." I hear the redhead's voice beyond the door, followed by Dan thanking her. A new wave of tears falls down my cheeks and my breathing grows more frenzied.

"Ally?" Dan calls to me, knocking on the door. I try to speak with a normal voice, but my throat is too tight and nothing leaves my mouth. "I know you're in there. Let me in."

The next thing I know, there's a rattling sound coming from the door handle. The lock is being picked. Light streams in as the door opens and I look up, my vision blurred from crying, but I can see enough to know how concerned Dan is.

He shuts the door, blocking out the party, and rushes to my side, kneeling in front of me. Dan strokes my hair back from my face, his eyes searching mine. "Shit. You're having a panic attack, aren't you?" He reaches for my purse, searching through it. "Do you have your medication with you?"

I shake my head, unable to talk, my chest heaving.

He grabs my hands and squeezes them gently. "Okay, Ally, everything is going to be all right. I'm going to take care of you, but you have to look at me and listen to what I say."

My eyes clench shut, filled with humiliation.

"Ally, baby, *look* at me."

The shock of Dan using such an affectionate nickname makes me open my eyes.

"We're going to try a breathing exercise," he says.

"Tried them. Never work."

"We don't have much else to try right now. I'm going to

count to four and I want you to inhale the whole time. Can you try that for me?"

I nod and he starts counting, his voice calm and soothing. We only make it to the count of one before I need to exhale. "Can't," I say, wincing.

"Yes, you can. Ally, look into my eyes and focus on me. Nothing else."

Dan begins counting again, his eyes soft and holding my gaze the entire time. I fail with the breathing again, but Dan continues encouraging me, never giving up, and slowly, I progress to inhaling over the count of two, fixated on those brown eyes and how they look at me. How he called me baby.

I make it to the count of three, focusing on the warmth of his hands spreading into me.

Four.

I think about all the times I've crawled into Dan's bed and slept in his arms.

My heartbeat has significantly slowed and my breathing is steady. The left side of Dan's lips lift into a grin and he whispers, "Amazing. You did it."

Because of him. I've never achieved these results without medication.

"Tell me what caused all of this."

I pull my hands free from his, wiping away fresh tears. "I shouldn't have come to this party. I don't know why I thought it would be a good idea. I'm not like you or any of the people here. I'm boring. I sit in my room and play the piano all day. I don't party. I don't have friends outside of the family. But you thrive in this setting, and it's easy to forget that there's a whole other side of you I don't know about. It makes me feel pathetic."

He looks at me incredulously, like I've said the most ridiculous thing. "Ally... You have no fucking clue, do you?"

"About what?"

"*You're* my person, remember? You get the real me. You're the *only* person who does. I have more fun spending the night at home with you than attending a party. You're the one person in this world that makes me feel understood. I can tell you things. Things I can't tell others. With you, I can relax and be me without feeling like I need to perform."

My heartbeat picks up, pounding over how special every word out of Dan's mouth is, and that he feels that way about *me*. He's so incredible and patient with me. "I feel all those things about you too. I'm sorry that you had to see me like this."

"I like that I've seen this side of you. I want to know every side of you, Ally. I like taking care of you. I want to always protect you and keep you safe." Dan reaches into his pocket and retrieves his neon deck of cards. He scans through them, stopping at the Queen of Hearts. "This belongs to you. You're my Queen of Hearts. Never forget it." He places her in my hand, returning the rest of the deck to his pocket.

The tears fall harder as I stare down at the card, understanding everything Dan's words don't say. This card, the Queen of Hearts, feels like a love confession between two people who can't be in love. I'm not pleased about the panic attack, but in some sense, I'm glad it happened, bringing this added closeness between us.

"You'll have an incomplete deck," I tell him, wiping my eyes. It's almost been a year since I gifted him these cards, and he has them on him constantly, always shuffling.

"I never play with this deck. It's too special. Every time I shuffle it, I think of you."

I smile, gazing down at the Queen of Hearts then back up at Dan. "I won't ever let go of it."

The Third Year

Obsession

Chapter 10

Ally

One year later, Saturday, September 20

Everyone in the audience is applauding me. An entire room full of people in their finest attire are smiling my way with approval. They all loved my performance.

I stand from the piano, brushing out the pink tulle of my dress and take a bow. My parents join me on either side, and we pose for a photo that will be on the front page of every newspaper tomorrow, reporting on the success of tonight's Forever Families benefit. We're at the Central Park Boathouse and this is the first time I've been asked to perform at one of these events. It's both exhilarating and nerve-wracking, being such a focal point of attention tonight.

Dozens of camera flashes go off. A male reporter joins us, speaking into a microphone, "Amabella, we hear Ally is in her senior year of high school and intends to audition for a spot at Juilliard next year."

"Yes. We're going to have our very own concert pianist one day in Ally. We're very proud of her," Mom responds, wrapping an arm around my shoulder and placing a kiss on my forehead. "We're proud of all our children and their accomplishments."

"Ally, it's been just you and your mother for so long. How are you adjusting to life with four stepbrothers and a stepfather?" The reporter holds the microphone up to me, waiting for my answer.

I like accepting praise from the public. Answering questions is a different story. I'm always fearful of saying the wrong thing or my words being interpreted in a way I didn't intend. It's happened before and I know it will happen again at some point.

"I love it," I answer, smiling and trying to sound confident. Forever Families is a noble cause, and as a Blackwood, I'm a part of the organization's face. It's just as important to me as it is to my parents to set a good example of a loving family and home. "I don't see any of them as stepfamily. Josh is a father to me. Dan, Killian, Tyler, and Felix are my brothers." My tummy flutters as I speak those words. The sensation travels lower, between the tops of my thighs.

I slept in Dan's bed again last night. I often sleep in his bed, but it was the first time he's done more than just hug me. The feeling of his hot palm still lingers on my skin, the way it slid up beneath my shirt and cupped my breasts. I wasn't wearing a bra. He had full access to my chest and I'm still tingling over the way his fingers brushed over my nipples. I didn't realize nipples could be so pleasurable. I moaned at the unexpected sensation, unintentionally arching my spine. My ass pressed back, and another startled sound left me when I felt how hard Dan was.

"Don't do that," Dan groaned against the nape of my neck when I started grinding. His free hand clutched my hips, pressing my ass firm to his cock but not allowing me to move. *"We really should go to sleep. I couldn't resist one feel. I haven't jerked off in days. Goodnight, Queen."*

My eyes flew wide open in the dark room, hearing such a raw confession when sex has always seemed like such an off-limits topic for us. I felt like I was about to spontaneously combust, I was that hot from the thought of Dan jerking off. With much struggle, I ended up falling asleep hours later.

The memory turns into a pulsing ache deep within my crotch. My head is a fevered mixture of lust and shame. I scan the crowd of guests at the benefit, my gaze landing on Dan. His eyes are already on me, though I doubt he's thinking about last night. It probably wasn't a big deal for him, feeling my breasts or talking about masturbating. He's been with lots of girls. I'm the virgin here who gets wet over the tiniest, most meaningless things.

Dan leaves his spot, and my eyes follow as he weaves through the crowd, walking farther away from me until I lose all sight of him. I don't know where he's heading; all I know is I want to be there with him instead of answering questions for the media.

I whisper into my mother's ear, "Can I please be excused for the bathroom?"

"Yes, darling," she murmurs, then turns back to Josh and the reporter and continues speaking with them.

I gather my sheet music from the piano, along with the neon Queen of Hearts card. I told Dan I wouldn't let go of her, and I meant it. She comes everywhere with me, tucked away in my purse. Tonight, I propped her up on the piano stand to calm my nerves for my performance.

"Great performance, Ally," Tyler calls as soon as I've stepped away from the limelight of cameras. I turn, finding him and his girlfriend, Harper, among the crowd, sharing a champagne at a high table.

They're an attractive couple, both twenty-two. Tyler is always clean-cut, constantly dressed in suits and with his dark hair gelled back. Harper has long scarlet curls and exudes elegance. They're nice people and always very welcoming to me. I don't know much about either of them other than Tyler is studying business, Harper is a dancer with the New York City Ballet, and the pair stick to themselves at family events, having some issue with Felix no one can figure out. I assume they're only here tonight for Mom's sake.

"Thank you. Are you two enjoying the evening?" My question is too formal, but I'm unsure of what else to say to them.

"It's lovely," Harper says, her focus on the items in my hands. "Hey, isn't that one of Dan's cards?"

I look down and realize she's referring to the Queen of Hearts. My skin is instantly clammy at the thought of anyone piecing together why I have this card and what it symbolizes. "Oh, um, yes. I found it on the ground earlier. Dan must have dropped it. I should return it to him. Excuse me."

I race off, heading in the direction Dan went, having no clue if I'll find him. The Boathouse is packed with people. I glance all around, searching, scanning the crowd, not spotting him anywhere until I step outside to a lonely section of the terrace opening out to the water.

He's leaning one shoulder against the brick wall, typing

something on his phone. A lock of dark hair hangs over his forehead. He's recently graduated from high school and when I think back to the sixteen-year-old guy Dan was when I first met him, he looks so mature. His shoulders are wider, his muscles thick and defined from frequent gym sessions with his brothers. He has a thick layer of stubble. There's a one-year age gap between us but I feel like such a girl beside him, instead of a woman.

Dan looks up, finding me, and places his phone in his suit pocket. "I was just texting you to join me, Queen."

I smile at the name he's taken to calling me in private ever since the night of my panic attack at that beach party. I adore the affection in his voice every time he speaks it. Tonight however, the affection is mixed with something else. His voice is deeper, much like the groan from last night when I pressed my ass against his dick.

His gaze trails down my body, lingering on my breasts and hips. "Did you wear that dress for me?"

My chest swells with a heavy breath, liking the way he looks at my body. How he doesn't attempt to hide that he's admiring me. No one is close enough to witness any of this interaction but we're out in the open and he really shouldn't be looking at me like this.

"You know I did." I shouldn't have said that either. I'm too consumed with thoughts of last night to care.

His eyes flick back up to mine and he studies me for a long moment as if trying to decipher something. "The things you said to that reporter were pretty fucked up. Calling me your brother."

"I've called you my brother before and you didn't have an issue with it. I think maybe you even liked it."

I don't know what possesses me to say such a thing or why I say it with such a sweet tone. Sometimes I flirt with

Dan, taunting him that I'm his little sister, and it's weird. I don't understand any of it or why I like it.

Dan's gaze narrows on me and his jaw tics. A moment later, he laughs beneath his breath. "Such a good little girl in public, aren't you. You better hope no one sees in you what I'm starting to."

My muscles clench, the feelings in my chest battling it out between arousal and fear of being publicly disgraced over my feelings for Dan. "What are you starting to see?"

"A repressed virgin who doesn't like the taste of vanilla. You have kinks I haven't figured out yet, but I think I'm close, little sis."

Heat bursts through me, every inch of my skin hot with embarrassment, yet my pulse is throbbing between my legs. This conversation feels dangerous. Dan can be so gentle with me at times and then I get this opposite side of him that's blunt and inappropriate, and all I want is to see more.

"Whatever you're implying, you're wrong," I tell him.

"Maybe, but I don't think so. You're always the role model daughter. Your mother's precious girl. That's what you've been your entire life. It's the role you're playing now with Forever Families. It makes you feel liked and accepted by people. But I think you get off on doing the wrong thing."

"And what's the wrong thing?"

"It's what you and I have been doing since the first moment we met. You like dressing pretty for your step-brother. Sneaking into my bed. Grinding against my cock. I wonder what else you'd like doing with me. I bet you think about fucking me most days, don't you?"

"Every day," I whisper.

His lips slowly curl into a smirk. "See? I'm figuring you out. Not as sweet as you appear. Beneath all the ribbons and bows, there's a little slut."

"A slut?" I repeat, startled and confused. Part of me feels like I should be offended, but the way he spoke the word sounded like praise.

"Yes. You're both my slut and my Queen of Hearts. I just haven't unlocked the two sides of you yet. Give it time and I will." He pushes off the wall to return inside, his hot breath grazing my ear as he passes me and whispers, "You look really pretty tonight, sis."

I watch him leave, rendered speechless over our conversation. It's not lost on me how Dan called me *his* slut. Is he implying we'll have sex in the future? We can't do that, no matter how much I want to. I wouldn't ever live down the humiliation if anyone found out, not to mention the disgrace it would throw upon Forever Families.

He's wrong about everything else he said too, about my sexual desires. How can Dan know any of those things about me when I don't know them about myself? I don't know a thing about sex other than what I've seen in movies. I've never even had an orgasm. I've touched myself a few times and it feels good, but a climax never happens. I don't know what I'm doing or how to get there.

There was one time I thought maybe I could come. Thoughts of having sex with Dan had entered my mind. It felt wrong to be thinking of him in such a moment. I stopped immediately, ashamed of touching myself over him.

Now, as I stand alone on the Boathouse terrace, I'm starting to question everything I believed of myself. Maybe Dan *is* right and that's why touching myself felt so good when I thought of him, because maybe I do get off on doing the wrong thing.

I'm desperate to experience how good I can make myself feel. But having an orgasm over my stepbrother is something I *definitely* shouldn't do.

Chapter 11

Dan

One month later, Tuesday, October 17

A NEW KINK

"You're smart, Daniel. Why don't you go to college and make something of your life instead of messing around playing poker? You're not a kid anymore." My father's scolding goes through one ear and out the other as he paces around the living room in our Manhattan apartment, late on a Monday night.

I slump into the couch cushions, staring out the window at the city lights. I hear this speech at least once a week since I graduated high school a couple months back, and it's getting stale.

He isn't pleased with how I've decided to make my money at the poker table, all because it tarnishes the reputation of his and Amabella's nonprofit organization. I try to keep my business out of the tabloids for my parents' sake, especially the games that aren't legal, but the media follow me around like mad.

My father always tells me I should have more direction like my brothers. Killian has moved out of our home and is training to be an athlete, Tyler is studying business with plans to be involved in Dad's old hotel business and has a serious, long-term girlfriend in Harper, and Felix owns a successful cocktail lounge. Dad is proud of them and the fine example they're setting in the public eye.

I rub a hand over my mouth, smothering a laugh. If he only knew the shit Felix gets up to beneath that "cocktail lounge" is ten times worse than anything I've done. But my oldest brother is better at keeping his vices hidden than I am.

"Are you playing poker just to defy me?"

"Pissing you off is an added benefit, but it's not why I play."

"Daniel, I have had enough of your attitude," he shouts. "I provide you with a home. I sent you to an excellent school. Growing up, you've had every luxury you could ever ask for. Yet you don't appreciate any of it. If you're so against me, you don't need my support any longer. I want you out of this apartment within the month. You're nineteen now. You can pay your own way and take care of your own life. Perhaps this will force you to start acting like a man."

My eyes dart to him and I sit up straight, snapping back at him. "You think I stay under your roof because I'm reliant on you for financial and parental support? I stay because Ally and Amabella mean something to me. You're not the incredible family man you think you are. It's all an act ever since Amabella has come into the picture. If you really cared, you would have been present in my life before you met her. You've always had some fucked up issue with me because of—"

Even in this moment, I can't bring myself to mention my mother's death. The guilt is heavy in my chest, knowing that my mere existence in this world has fucked up all the lives around me. The question of *what if she'd never died* always weighs on me.

My brothers and I would have grown up in a loving household. My father would have been around a lot more instead of running off to deal with his grief. Maybe I would have had a proper relationship with my father. So would my brothers.

"You know what? Fuck this shit. I'll happily move out." I turn my back on the argument and head for my room. My father calls after me, demanding I sit back down, but I ignore every word.

As soon as I enter my room, my eyes catch on the neon deck of cards sitting on my bedside table. I lay on the bed and start shuffling, irritated and trying to calm myself. I turn on a neon lamp for its calming effects too, this one a dark purple.

Not even a minute later, the front door of the penthouse opens and I hear Amabella and Ally greet my father on their return from Ally's piano lesson. He mentions my name to them with frustration but I can't hear the specifics.

The next thing I know, Ally barges into my bedroom, hands on her hips and glaring at me. Despite the anger on her face, my mind turns to filth, the way it always does when I see her in her school uniform. The knee-high socks and short dress. The pink satin ribbon she always weaves through her blond hair. With the purple neon light emphasizing her silhouette, she looks like a wet dream.

"You *can't* move out," she says. "We'll never see each other."

"I'll take you with me."

Her anger morphs into shock. The words slipped out of my mouth in haste, the idea of moving out with Ally unplanned but sounding more appealing with each passing second.

I'll pay for her senior year at school if I need to. I make shitloads from my poker winnings, which my father can't stand, to the extent that he cut me off from receiving the trust fund I was meant to inherit when I turned eighteen, like he was trying to punish me.

I'm glad I don't have his money. I don't want to be indebted to the man at all.

Before Ally can say anything, Amabella's voice cuts through the walls, startling both of us. "Josh, you are *not* kicking Dan out of our home." Dad tries to reason with her, but barely gets a word out. "Dan has become my son too. I don't even want to think about the impact this will have on Ally. You didn't see what she was like before she met him. As a mother, it was terrible to witness. Their friendship is the best thing that has ever happened to her."

Ally and I look at each other. She licks her lips, blushing over her mother's words. Amabella is an angel for the way she treats me, which only deepens the guilt surrounding my feelings for her daughter. If she only knew *how* close Ally and I are, I'm sure she'd be all for kicking me out.

"I'm still in school," Ally says quietly. A plea. "I'm not moving out of my home. Plus, if *we* moved out together, it would look... wrong. Please, don't leave me."

My chest warms at those last words. *Please, don't leave me.* When she speaks like that... It's so vulnerable and desperate and... I am so weak for this girl. There's nothing I wouldn't do for her.

I've never experienced such intense feelings for a girl, as I do with Ally. There are delicate and sentimental moments between us, then raw truths like our conversation at the Boathouse that make me want to uncover how twisted her deepest desires are.

I haven't pushed Ally for more since that night of the benefit a month ago. I could see on her face how turned on yet embarrassed she was. She's caught up in what is "right" and "wrong" and I don't want to make her do anything she isn't ready for.

I sigh, knowing any plan to move out of home with Ally is far-fetched. She's right—living together wouldn't look great. So far, no one has questioned our friendship and "sibling bond." But they would if it were just the two of us living together. If rumors spread to the paparazzi, they'd have a field day, which Ally wouldn't handle well.

She's been slandered in the media a couple of times since joining the Blackwood family. Ally can't shrug off the negative attention as well as the rest of us can. I suppose it's a sensitive area, considering the bullying she's been victim to in the past.

"Fine, I won't leave," I mutter, mindlessly shuffling the deck of cards.

"Thank you."

"But as soon as you graduate, I'm leaving this place."

She frowns. "I guess all good things have to end."

Though her words are cryptic, I know she's referring to this set up we have here, the two of us constantly being around each other. Most nights, secretly sharing a bed.

All of that will disappear once we're not living together.

I'm not ready to say goodbye to all these moments.

"Siblings *do* move out of the house together. It's not that unheard of." I don't know who I'm trying to convince here. Yes, siblings can move out together, but often for short periods of time. Not years on end.

Ally doesn't say anything in response, and I know it's because she's not eager to leave home. She enjoys living here with our parents and having a family. Ally likes the stability and love my father gives her. He takes an interest in her hobbies. When I'm not around for Ally to hang out with, she spends time with him and Amabella, doing cutesy little family things like playing charades or having popcorn movie nights.

Ally walks through our shared bathroom to her bedroom, leaving the doors open so we can talk as she unpacks her school bag. "You know I'm auditioning for Juilliard."

Of course, I know. Studying the piano at Juilliard is a dream of Ally's. She wants to be a concert pianist. It's all she ever talks about.

"If I get in next year, I'll be a full-time student. It's not an ideal financial situation to be moving out now."

I step up to her room, leaning one hand high on the doorframe. She's about to receive the first part of her trust fund from Dad. She could live off that money, but I don't bother suggesting the idea, knowing she'll be sensible and leave it untouched.

"I can pay for anything you want," I say, watching Ally slip out of her shoes.

"I want my own money."

"You're asking me to stay here with my father for years? Fuck, Ally." She knows I'll do it for her. That's how whipped I am, for a girl I've never even kissed. I groan, rubbing a hand over my face. "I need to go for a drive to blow off some steam."

"Shuffling cards hasn't helped?"

There's a teasing sound to her words. I give a humorless laugh.

"I'll come with you. I don't like you driving when you're angry. Let me change out of my school uniform."

Before I have the chance to give Ally privacy, she unzips her school dress and lets it fall to the ground, revealing a matching set of pink lingerie beneath. I stiffen at the sight of her near-naked body and how casually she's treating this moment.

Ally has never undressed in front of me before, at least not with the lights on. I've seen her in a bikini but that was different. The whole family was around. This moment, it's just for us. She's admitted to dressing for my pleasure, and it stirs up something possessive deep within me, knowing the thong and bra she's wearing was picked out for me. Her bra is so sheer I can see her nipples.

Exercising self-control, I lean against the door frame and watch Ally search through her wardrobe in silence, the two of us never making eye contact or acknowledging her indecency. After all, this isn't how step siblings are supposed to behave. I don't try to hide how hard I am. I just admire the perfect curve of her breasts and her ass in that thong while questioning what the real meaning of this moment is about for her. What it's about for me.

Ally knows what she's doing right now is wrong, and I'm certain that's why she's doing it. She likes teasing me, that much has been clear for a while. Her intensions aren't cruel. She's not falsely leading me on. I can tell the teasing is Ally's way of expressing her repressed desires. It's her way of being with me.

This display is taking things to another level, and I file away the image of her body for later when I jerk off. She has to know I jerk off over her. I'm sure she likes that I do.

I told her she has kinks. I'm starting to realize I do too, because I want to fuck her right now but not in the way I've fucked other girls. With them, it's always been just sex. Plain, regular, even boring sex, when I come to think of it.

Watching Ally flaunt herself in front of me, I feel something new within myself. Something I've never felt toward any other girl. A possessive, dominant side. I'm so close to telling Ally to lay on the bed and spread her legs, then instructing her to pull her panties aside, showing me how pretty her cunt is. I want to sit back and enjoy the sight of Ally while commanding her, telling her exactly what to do with her body and how to make her pussy feel good. Then I want to order her to sit on my dick because she wants it, knowing how wrong it is. I want to be the one to teach her everything about sex.

She's slowly exploring her sexuality and learning what she likes. I think I'm learning something new about myself too, and it's clear I'm developing an obsession with watching my stepsister, pushing her boundaries, and making her do all the filthy things she doesn't want to admit turn her on.

Ally slips a dress over her head, finally meeting my gaze with an innocent smile, like nothing inappropriate has just happened between us. Fucking little brat. The good girl act only turns me on more.

"Will you zip me up?" she says so sweetly.

I step behind Ally, slowly raising the zip, my fingers lingering on the fabric, on the warm skin at the nape of her neck when I'm done. All the impulses I have with this girl, I shouldn't act upon any of them. She isn't ready for what I want to do to her. More importantly, she's my stepsister and I shouldn't cross the line with her more than I already have.

Doing the right thing, I grab my keys from my pocket. "Let's go, Queen."

Chapter 12

Ally

Four months later, Saturday, March 3

Saturday night and I'm at home in a satin nightgown, practicing my Juilliard audition piece, when a knock on my bedroom door interrupts me. "Yeah?"

The door opens and Dan leans against the frame, grinning at me. "Sounding good."

I love that smile. I swear he gets more handsome with each day.

"Just wanted to let you know I'm home in case you decide to take a break and want to watch a movie with me," he says. "Or I can help with your audition."

My audition is in one week and has been a major cause of stress. I can perform all day, in front of anyone, anywhere, but I have a mental block when it comes to auditioning. My therapist tells me, as with most issues in my life, the mental block stems from the domestic violence we lived with—being in a stressful environment and feeling trapped.

Whenever I audition, the nerves take control of me. My fingers don't move with fluency. Sometimes, I forget which notes to play. Worst case scenario, I have a panic attack. It's happened twice before.

It can't happen again for my Juilliard audition.

Dan has been so amazing, talking me through my fears and helping me practice the breathing technique that worked so well the night of the beach party. The panic attacks have been happening far less frequently, and thanks to Dan, I'm now able to self-regulate my emotions without medication when I feel an oncoming episode. I love how supportive Dan is and how he always believes in me.

I'm keen for a break from the piano and to watch a movie. In Dan's language, the movie invitation is code for *let me hold you while we watch a movie*. This is what we do each time we watch anything, just the two of us, and I never turn down an opportunity to be in Dan's arms.

He always holds me the way I imagine a boyfriend would, and I love it. I get butterflies in my tummy when I sit in his lap and his stubble brushes against my cheek. The scent of his cologne is hypnotic. Sometimes I'll even feel his erection on my back. I get wet from feeling his dick and knowing he's turned on.

Everything feels so adult and intense between us, even though we've never done anything sexual with each other. At least, that's how Dan makes *me* feel. For him, we're probably the definition of innocence, considering the amount of sex he's had.

"I thought you were out playing poker with Felix?"

"I finished early." He shrugs, sounding a little off. "I'm going to take a shower. So, you keen for a movie?"

Only now, when Dan reaches for the bathroom door handle, do I realize what's different about him. Dan's hair is ruffled. There's something red on his white collar. Lipstick.

My chest twists with jealousy. He wasn't out with Felix at all tonight. He was with a girl.

"Um... No movie tonight. I'm too busy to take a break." I keep the jealousy out of my voice because it has no place being there.

"Damn. Okay, the beautiful maestro is hard at work. I'll let you get back to it."

The door shuts and I collapse on my bed, screaming into a pillow. I'm not angry at Dan for having sex, if that's what he was doing earlier tonight. Our situation is complicated and we're in no way committed to each other. After his seventeenth birthday, I'm the one who insisted he continue sleeping around.

Since then, I've grown more attached to him and it's wrong. Everything about us is wrong, from the way he calls me his queen, to how I sleep in his bed and undress in front of him. I shouldn't do any of those things. But the way Dan makes me feel, I can't stop myself. At least we're not having sex; that's how I justify my behavior.

If I had the ability to talk to other guys, I'd be trying to date them to expel this sexual frustration Dan fills me with. But the depressing truth is I'm eighteen, a virgin, and awkward as hell around the opposite sex.

I hear the shower turn on, and sigh, removing the pillow from my face. Dan is cleaning up, probably so I don't smell the scent of sex on him. My mind wanders to thoughts of what Dan did tonight with that girl, whoever she is.

What does he think about while having sex? That the girl is beautiful? That he can't get enough of her body? That he needs her and that the act of making her come is all it takes to make him finish? Does he use protection, or does he get off on coming inside her without a condom?

I can't take the thoughts for a second longer. They're pure agony. I have never hated something more in my life. I want him to know what he does to me. How fucked up I am over needing him but never having him. I want him to be so goddamn obsessed with me that he never looks at another girl again. It's just me he sees and fucks and comes inside of. My God, I want him to come inside of me so fucking badly. I want it dripping down my legs.

My hand slips beneath my panties, too overcome by the constant ache between my thighs to care that what I'm about to do is wrong. I let my mind wander to those nights we share a bed, with his hand fastened around my waist.

Giving in to the fantasy, I imagine that his hand moves lower. I think about Dan's hot breath on my neck, his voice whispering dirty things into my ear, telling me how much he wants me and how he'd give anything to be inside me.

The bathroom door opens and I pull my hand out of my panties at lightning speed, hot with embarrassment when I see Dan standing in the doorway. He's wearing black track pants with no shirt, his brown hair is damp, and he's busy hanging his towel on the towel rack.

A rush of relief fills me when I realize he didn't catch me touching myself.

Dan finishes with the towel and looks at me. "You sure I can't tempt you with a movie—" His gaze narrows on me, curious and studying, finding me on my back, propped on my elbows with my nightgown hiked up.

I'm wrong. He does know. Dan stares at my cheeks which are flushed with the evidence of what I've just been doing. His gaze darkens, his jawline stiffening, and I think I'm about to die with humiliation.

"Don't stop." The words leave his mouth, low and gravelly, and are the last thing I expected to hear.

"I wasn't..." I can't finish the sentence. I'm pinned beneath his gaze, unable to move.

He swallows hard, the muscles in his throat straining. "Giving yourself an orgasm?"

I'm so hot that I can't speak. My heart is pounding like I've never experienced before, pumping adrenaline all through my body. Slowly, I shake my head to answer Dan's question, my gaze never leaving his. "I don't know how. I've never..."

"You've never had an orgasm?"

"I've tried before. I can never get myself there unless I think of..." I won't allow myself to speak his name out loud. Though, I get the sense he can tell where my answer was heading. "It feels... wrong."

"That's the whole fun of it." A flicker of amusement enters his voice. "I think deep down, you like doing the wrong thing. Why resist it? The more wrong it is, the better it feels, Ally."

Hearing him speak my name makes my clit pulse so hard that I clench my legs.

He contemplates me for a long moment with torment in his eyes. I've caught him looking at me many times over the years with desire, but this is something different. It's dangerous and starved, like he's been pushed beyond breaking point. My new favorite expression.

"Poor little thing," he finally says, his voice deep and smooth. "All this time, rubbing up against my dick in bed, letting me tease your perfect tits. You must be so backed up. And you don't even know how to relieve yourself. I fuck my fist like crazy over you."

"You do?" I murmur.

"Every day. Let me teach you how to take care of your-self, little sister."

My pussy tightens, hearing the label Dan just used for me in this moment of all. I realize how true his previous statement is. *The more wrong it is, the better it feels.* I must be really fucked up in the head because I've never felt more alive than in this moment. I've never wanted some-thing so much as what he's describing. For *Dan* to teach me.

But fear makes me hesitate. "Our parents are home. They're in the next room over."

"Then I guess you'll have to be quiet." He groans, running a hand down his groin and drawing my attention to the tented erection in his pants.

I should have more common sense than to continue with this. Aside from it being wrong, this will change things between me and Dan going forward. Our friendship. Every-thing. Will I even be able to look at him the same without being flooded with embarrassment?

Those are all the thoughts that enter my mind, but none of them win against the way my body begs to be relieved after years of pent-up sexual tension.

"What do I do?" I whisper.

"Take your clothes off."

I stand from the bed, barely believing my actions and that I have the confidence to go through with this. But I do. Dan draws out a depraved side of me. He's always made me want to do things I shouldn't.

My hands shake as I push the nightgown straps off my shoulders. I let the dress drop to the floor, pooling around my feet and exposing my breasts as I stand in front of Dan.

I always expected to feel vulnerable and self-conscious being this naked in front of a guy, but the way Dan watches me has me feeling the opposite, like I'm the one person in this world who has power over him.

Dan groans when I slide my panties down, his gaze never faltering from my smooth pussy.

My heart races and I'm unsure what to do next, yet incredibly aroused. "Can we... turn the lights off?"

"No. I want to see all of you. Lie on the bed," he instructs. His voice is commanding, like nothing I've ever heard from him. It's intimidating yet at the same time, I like seeing this side of him. I like being his girl and for him to do what he wants with me, even if it's only for a few minutes. I trust Dan and can't imagine myself ever doing this with anyone else.

Following his words, I lie on my back.

Dan steps closer, the muscles in his arms flexing as he rests his hands on the footrail of my bed, watching me. "Stroke your clit."

I reach down, my hand trembling as I place my index finger on my clit and stroke.

"Use all of your fingers. Not just one."

I change my technique, a gasp leaving my lips at the added pleasure.

"Feel better?"

I nod, my fingers moving back and forth.

Dan watches me, his eyes fixed on my hand, his breath growing audible. "What's a thought that turns you on?"

"You, fucking me." I can't believe I spoke the fantasy out loud. But then again, I can't believe any of the things I'm doing in this moment. No point holding back now. "You, fucking *only* me. You want me and no one else. No other girl turns you on."

His gaze flicks to mine with disbelief, every muscle in his body freezing. "You think I'm attracted to other girls?"

My hand stops moving. "I know you are. You have sex—"

"Listen to me carefully, Ally," his voice comes out low but assertive. "Those other girls mean nothing. They're a distraction. A coping mechanism because I can't have you. You're the *only* one I want. You want me to stop seeing them? I will. I'll do *anything* to please you, Queen."

His words send a rush of pleasure through my core, exiting my body with a moan.

Dan smirks at my reaction. "Use your imagination. That's what I do. I think about you riding my dick and it gets me off every time."

My hips buck at that visual, my clit desperately seeking out friction after hearing Dan's confession. I continue rubbing, needing release from the throbbing ache deep within me.

He wants me. Only me.

He jerks off to the thought of only me.

He'll stop sleeping with the other girls.

"Fuck. Look at you. Desperate little thing. That's it, Ally," Dan purrs. "Move your hand faster. Imagine my cock filling you up, stretching you out. Feel how good it is."

I close my eyes, picturing Dan's strong body pressing against mine, his cock sliding deep inside me. I can imagine his fingers gripping my hips, and his breath hot on my neck. My hand moves faster, my breathing becoming more jagged.

The fantasy sends shivers of arousal through me, building with intensity, and more sounds leave my lips that I never knew I was capable of. I lose myself to the moment, shedding all embarrassment and following what feels good. My hand moves even faster, my hips lifting off the bed in time with my fingers. My heart is hammering in my chest and sweat breaks out on my forehead.

"You're getting close, aren't you?" Dan asks, his voice husky. I open my eyes, finding just how pained and tormented he looks, and loving it. "Slow down, I'm not through with our lesson yet."

I follow his guidance, feeling the pleasure of what must be an oncoming orgasm back off.

"Keep rubbing your clit. Take your other hand and slide your fingers inside your pussy."

I gasp at his direction, never having done this to myself before, but I obey, being so needy, and slowly slide a finger into my wet entrance. The feeling is foreign and intense, drawing another moan from me.

"I can only imagine how tight you are. Put another finger in," he commands, his words firm.

It's a tight fit, but I manage to slide another finger inside. Pleasure courses through me at the fullness, making my pussy clench around my fingers.

"Three," he says, growing more insistent.

I push a third finger inside, feeling my resistance fading with each finger.

"Spread yourself open. Show me how wet you are," he instructs.

I do as he says and gain so much satisfaction as Dan's eyes widen at the sight, his breath catching in his throat.

"So fucking hot," he murmurs, his hands fisted around the footrail. "Keep going, Ally. Fuck yourself with your hand. Show me how much you want this."

I do as he says, my fingers moving in and out of my wetness while stroking my clit. My gaze remains on Dan, every now and then trailing down to his hard cock and wishing it would replace my hand.

"Now it's time to make yourself feel truly good," he says. "Go faster and squeeze your pussy tight around your fingers."

I do, purposefully clenching my inner muscles, and an unexpected cry of pleasure leaves my lips.

Dan hushes me, fighting a grin as he glances at the door. "You don't want our parents hearing what we're doing in here, do you?"

"Ally?" My mom calls out, and I go instantly still with horror. She could walk in on us at any second. I didn't lock the door. How could I be so stupid? "Are you okay?"

Dan's eyes are back on me, his voice stern. "Don't you dare stop fucking your fingers. Answer her."

"I'm fine," I call out, plunging my fingers into my pussy as I fight to keep my voice normal. My voice cracks at the very end but I don't think Mom notices. She doesn't say anything else, and I hear her footsteps disappear.

"Good girl," Dan says. "Let's practice squeezing again."

My pussy clenches and releases, building the tension of what I know must be an orgasm.

Dan watches me, his eyes never leaving my hand, his breathing ragged. "Such a quick learner. Now, imagine your pussy is squeezing around my cock. Can you imagine how good that would feel?"

"Yes," I whisper, my voice shaking. I can imagine it so clearly, his cock sliding inside me, hitting all the right spots.

"Are you enjoying this, Ally?" he asks.

I nod, my cheeks flushed and my breath coming quicker. "Yes. I've needed this for so long."

He swallows hard, watching my hand. "You want to come, don't you?"

"Yes."

Dan leaves his post at the foot of my bed and kneels on

the ground beside me, his fingers gently brushing my hair back from my face. "You're so beautiful, Ally. So sexy. I can't believe you've never done this to yourself."

I can't believe it either. I never knew I could feel this good.

"You're going to be doing this every day from now on, aren't you? Playing with your pussy. Making yourself feel good."

I nod.

"And each day, you're going to imagine my cock is filling you up. Imagine how good it would feel to have me inside you."

I start to see stars.

"Faster," he says, his voice like velvet.

My breathing quickens. My heart is racing and I lose myself in the pleasure, my body on fire.

"*Faster*, Ally. You're so close. I know you can do it."

Pure ecstasy bursts through my entire body and I cry out, having no control over how loud I am. Dan smirks, full of satisfaction as he covers my mouth with his hand, protecting us from being discovered. My body arches off the bed as the most intense sensations spread through me.

This is an orgasm? This is what I've been missing out on all these years? I'm addicted already. My pussy clenches so incredibly tight around my fingers, and my entire body shakes with pleasure.

As the waves of my orgasm begin to subside, I collapse back onto the bed, my breath coming in gasps.

Dan releases his hand from my mouth, and I look up at him in a daze. What we've just done together never should have happened, yet I can't bring myself to regret any of it. I love the way he praises me for doing something so wrong.

Dan stands up, the smirk gone, replaced with harsh

depravity. "Now that you know how to give yourself an orgasm, be a good girl and practice lots. Don't deprive yourself of what you need." He walks to the bathroom door, pausing with his hand on the doorknob as he looks back at me. "Don't enter my bed tonight, Ally. I won't be able to behave myself after what I just witnessed."

Chapter 13

Dan

One week later, Saturday, March 10

The moment I realize

We don't talk about that night, the one that happened a week ago. We both know it shouldn't have happened. Ally stopped sleeping in my bed altogether because she knows after that display, if we get too close, we'll give in and have sex. It was by far the hottest night of my life. There was no physical contact, but I got so much satisfaction from teaching Ally about her body and watching her enjoy herself. Sometimes, she catches me watching her throughout the day, mentally replaying the sight of her fingering herself. She always blushes and laughs, telling me to stop looking at her in that way.

I'm so addicted to that laugh. To everything about her.

"Alexandra Hastings?" a female assistant pops her head out of the Juilliard audition room, calling Ally's full name. "They're ready for you."

Ally stands from her chair beside me, stiff as anything. In one hand, she holds her sheet music, along with the neon Queen of Hearts. I love how she carries that card around with her everywhere and how she props it on the piano stand for courage when performing.

I rise from my chair too, taking her free hand in mine. No one sees the way I touch her. We're the only two people in this waiting room and the assistant is gone. Amabella and Dad wanted to be here for Ally, but she insisted it just be me since I've been such a help with her anxiety.

I stroke a lock of blond hair behind her ear and smile. "Hey, take a deep breath. You've got this. Show them how amazing you are on the piano."

She nods, weaving her fingers with mine. It's such a small gesture, yet so intimate that it sends warmth up my arm. "Thank you for being here," she says.

"I wouldn't be anywhere else."

Ally disappears into the audition room, closing the door behind her. I sit back in my chair, waiting patiently for her return. A few minutes of silence pass before I hear the familiar notes of Mozart's Sonata in A major that Ally has spent months perfecting.

I close my eyes, listening to her beautiful music. This tune has become a favorite piece of mine, and I laugh to myself, thinking about how I didn't know a thing about classical music before Ally came along, nor did I care to learn, and how this girl has infiltrated every aspect of my life.

The music comes to an abrupt end mid-song. My eyes flick open and my heart stops.

Fuck.

I cling to the hope that Ally's music resumes, that there's some positive explanation for the disruption. But as the seconds pass by in deafening silence, I know something has gone seriously wrong inside that audition room.

I'm on my feet in an instant, with my heart in my throat as I pace back and forth, contemplating how to respond. Does she need me in there? I won't enter and disrupt the audition unless I'm requested, but the thought of Ally breaking down and me standing back is tough to stomach. There's a large part of me praying I'm wrong about everything and I'm catastrophizing the situation.

The door opens behind me, and I spin around, finding the assistant escort Ally out of the audition room. I don't hear a word the lady says. Nothing around me registers except the tears streaming down Ally's face and the way my heart is breaking for her.

She's hyperventilating. Her face is red. I take Ally off the assistant's hands, asking her to give us privacy. The lady returns to the audition room as I sit Ally on a chair and kneel before her, telling her to focus on my eyes and take deep breaths while I count. It's the same routine we always run through, except this time it takes longer to calm her.

Ten minutes pass before I have Ally breathing properly, though the tears don't stop. "I'm sorry," she sobs.

"Ally, you have nothing to apologize for."

"I do. I thought I could get through the audition. I started feeling trapped and... I've let everyone down. Mom and Josh will be disappointed in me. It will be in the papers that I ran out of my audition with a panic attack. Worst of all, I've let you down."

I wipe her tears away with my thumbs. "You haven't disappointed anyone, especially not me."

"I have. You worked so hard to help me with my anxiety."

"Ally, I don't care about anything except your happiness. The audition didn't go well. Who gives a fuck. We'll keep practicing and you'll audition again. You're incredible. I know you can do this."

Another tear falls down her cheek. There's so much sadness in her beautiful blue eyes. Yet she gazes at me in silence, with such tenderness that it makes my heart leap. "You're the best person I've ever known," she whispers. "You do so much for me. You're my person. My everything. I wish I could do as much for you."

"Ally, just being you is everything I need." As I speak those words, I realize how true they are.

I don't need Ally to do anything for me other than be herself because I'm in love with everything she is. I love the girl who comes from a rough past. The dedicated musician. The girl who is shy around new people but not me. The girl who cares too much about me to let my birthday slip by unnoticed. The innocent virgin who has the confidence to get naked in front of me and do filthy things.

I've been in love with her for years, ever since that day after my seventeenth birthday when I told her she's my person. I just hadn't realized what these feelings meant until this moment.

I want to tell her right now that I love her, but it's not the right time. I don't know if it ever will be. Just because I say the words doesn't change our situation. We can't be together in any socially acceptable manner. More so for Ally—she's caught up in appearances and wanting to please everyone, and I respect that, but there's no space for an *us* in that equation.

So, I hold onto the confession, bringing the back of Ally's hand to my lips and placing a soft kiss on her skin. "Let's get you home, Queen."

The Fourth Year

Corruption

Chapter 14

Dan

Six months later, Monday, September 15

THE PLAN

Six months on from the night when I taught Ally how to give herself an orgasm and the memory is still constantly on my mind. I'll never forget the little sounds she made or the way her brows pinched together like the pleasure was too much for her to handle. How her hips bucked and rose off the bed as she climaxed.

I think about that night again now as I lay on Ally's bed, shuffling my neon cards while watching her play the piano. She's in a world of her own and it's beautiful seeing her like this. I'm mesmerized by everything this girl does. Even the simple things have me in a trance, like whenever she speaks my name. The way she hums her favorite songs. Even the way she fucking breathes.

"Beethoven would not be proud of me for how I just

played his concerto," Ally says once her fingers come to a stop.

"Sounded perfect to me, Queen."

She glances over her shoulder at me, sighing with a laugh. "You think everything I play is perfect."

That laugh. I feel it in my dick. I'm lost in the way her blue eyes linger on me. Ally must sense it, because she leaves the piano and joins me on her bed, sitting right next to me with her legs draped over mine.

"It wasn't perfect," she says, so casually, as if her thigh isn't resting against my dick.

My card shuffling stops. I grab her hips and pull her closer, not caring if she feels how hard she's making me. I place my palm on the inside of her bare thigh, my thumb brushing beneath the hem of her skirt. Fuck, I love that she lets me hold her like this. I always wonder how far I can push my luck. If my hand keeps rising beneath Ally's skirt, at what point will she stop me? Will she let my fingers slip under her panties?

My better judgment tells me not to test Ally's limits. She still hasn't returned to my bed at night. She has reservations about us doing anything too physical. She won't even acknowledge that she got naked in front of me. It's not our dynamic.

Ally likes to pretend she's not a total fucking slut for me.

That's our dynamic.

The night of Ally's first orgasm, it was like some sexual awakening in her. Sometimes, when our parents aren't around, I'll hear Ally in her bedroom, moaning as she pleases herself, practicing what I taught her. She wants me to hear, otherwise, she would keep the volume down. Her orgasms sound intense. Each time, I end up fucking my fist while I listen. I'm sure that's what gets her off, knowing how much I want her.

On one occasion, Ally showered with the bathroom door ajar, just enough for me to peer in and watch her hold the detachable shower head to her pussy. I don't know if that door was left open on purpose as an invitation for me to watch her.

Mistake on Ally's behalf or not, I *did* watch her through the crack, very well knowing I shouldn't. Not once had she ever left the door open before that night. She wants the world to perceive her as the perfect daughter of Josh and Amabella Blackwood. The face of Forever Families. But Ally secretly gets off on being naughty. She's a dirty little thing for me and only me, and I love it.

Outside of those moments, our lives continue as normal. That's the dance we play. It's what makes my dick leak all the more for her.

"The song needs to be perfect for Juilliard." She exhales loudly, her words sad.

Ally isn't auditioning this year, wanting more control over her anxiety before applying to Juilliard again. She recently graduated from high school and has made a plan with our parents to take a gap year and focus on her piano skills, along with attending weekly therapy sessions to get a hold on her anxiety surrounding auditions. She works so incredibly hard to achieve her goals, it's an inspiration.

"Let's practice the breathing technique again." Ally draws her legs away from me, crossing them as she sits up straight in a meditative position.

She looks so damn pretty as she closes her eyes and tries to center herself. Her lips are slightly parted. A pink headband pushes her blond hair back from her face.

After a few moments, when I haven't moved or said

anything, she pops an eye open to check what I'm doing and finds me unapologetically watching her.

"What?" She smiles, playfully shoving my chest. "Come on, talk me through the counting."

"You don't need me to count for you. You've got this."

"Yeah, but I like the sound of your voice." She closes her eyes again, and I give in, hearing her speak like this.

I talk her through the exercise, with my eyes remaining open the entire time so I can admire the sight of her sitting in front of me.

Sometimes, Ally talks about an alternative path to getting into Juilliard. There's a famous pianist in Paris named DeLacroix. Ally says he's incredible and offers a scholarship to one student each year where he teaches at the Paris Conservatoire. The scholarship isn't for a college degree but a one-year steppingstone course. It would add to Ally's skill and make her a more desirable candidate for Juilliard.

She tells me it would be a dream to be a recipient of the scholarship. That some of the greatest musicians of all time have graduated from this school. She doesn't have the courage to apply for the scholarship, but I know she wants it. Her face lights up every time she talks about studying in Paris.

When we finish the breathing exercise, her eyes slowly open and a relaxed smile spreads over her pretty lips I've envisioned kissing a million times. I'd give anything to kiss Ally right now.

Instead, I make a decision that will perhaps one day show Ally how much she means to me. I'm going to send the Paris Conservatoire an audition tape on Ally's behalf. My little secret. I'll take a recording of her playing the piano when she's unaware. That's when she's at her most brilliant, pouring herself into her music.

She'll get the scholarship. I know she will. Then she'll have options. If she decides to accept the scholarship, fuck, I'll move to Paris too. I'll give everyone some believable excuse as to why I need to travel with her. All I want is the best for Ally. I want to give her everything.

Chapter 15

Ally

Nine months later, Friday, June 1

<small>A NEW TOY TO PLAY WITH</small>

There's a package sitting on my bed when I return home late at night after dinner with my uncle Daxton.

A discreet package.

My cheeks flush with embarrassment, imagining my mother accepting this package from the delivery man and placing it on my bed, not knowing what's inside. I still can't believe I ordered this thing online.

It was one night last week when I was tossing and turning in bed, unable to sleep because I was so sexually frustrated, underwhelmed by the orgasm I'd given myself. I give myself orgasms daily, like Dan told me to all those months ago right before I auditioned for Juilliard. But my fingers have stopped being enough. I want to be fucked and to feel full. I caved in and ordered a dildo, blushing the entire time I placed the order.

No guy is going to satisfy my needs except the one guy I can't have. I'm sure, if I applied myself, I could find a boyfriend, or at the very least, someone to take my virginity. But neither of those options are appealing unless the guy is Dan. And sex with Dan isn't an option, as much as I want it to be.

This toy will have to make do.

I unwrap the box, my tummy fluttering as I hold the dildo. Using this dildo feels sordid and way too adult for me and... my pussy clenches at the thought of the orgasm this thing could give me.

I look at the toy's instructions, wondering if the device is as amazing as the reviews say. Apparently, it does everything. The device is multi-functional, with different speeds, rotation patterns, and has a remote control. It has a suction cup base for mounting different surfaces, is waterproof, and even has an ejaculation function.

Being the only one home right now, I take advantage of the privacy and drop my panties. Lying on the bed, I lift my dress over my hips. The anticipation already has me soaked, so I place the head of the toy to my opening and slowly push inside, not utilizing any of its functions yet.

The dildo is big. Too big for me and already stings with just the tip inside. I've always heard sex can be painful for girls during their first time. I've only ever had my fingers inside me, and they have nothing on the size of this dildo.

Determined to get the pain over with so I can enjoy the toy quicker, I push deeper, wincing at the unpleasant experience and needing to brace myself with slow breaths. When I can't take anymore, I pull the dildo out and sit up in disappointment. There's blood. On my legs. On the toy. I knew to expect this, I just didn't realize sex would be this painful.

Feeling foolish, like I'm some silly little girl playing with toys I shouldn't, I give up and bring the dildo to the shower with me to clean up. I turn the water on and stand beneath the downpour, washing away the blood, telling myself I'll try again another night. That hopefully next time it won't hurt.

Right as I turn the water off, a buzzing sound startles me. I look at the toy on the soap rack, seeing the head rotate in small circles.

"You bought a toy."

I gasp, wiping away a small patch of fog on the glass shower wall, finding Dan leaning against the doorframe of my bedroom with the dildo's remote control in his hand. Thank God he's the one who found the remote and not my parents. Though, I'm still hot with embarrassment.

"I thought you were out tonight," I say.

A look of contemplation sits in his eyes. I'm burning up, dying to know what thoughts are running through his mind. "I wanted to come home and watch a movie with you." Dan pauses, his brows drawn together as he studies the remote. "But now there's something I want to do even more."

Heat rushes between my thighs and a heavy pulse comes to life in my clit at the thought of what he could be implying.

"Fuck, Ally. Tell me to leave right now. Tell me you don't want me anywhere near you, because finding you with this toy... *fuck*. There's not a trace of decency in me tonight."

My heart pounds so hard I can feel it. The dark look in his eyes, the rough tone of his voice, I've only truly seen this side of him once before, when he taught me how to touch myself. It's a dangerous side, yet I think it might be my favorite. I should do as Dan says and tell him to leave. This interaction between us isn't appropriate. He's giving me a chance to stop this, being honest about his indecent intentions.

But I don't want Dan's composed side. I want the dominant side who tells me what to do with my body and praises me for it. The side of Dan I spend every day desperately wanting to see again.

"Ally..." Dan warns as the seconds pass and I remain silent. "Tell me to leave."

"No."

His eyes remain fixed on me for a long moment, fighting an internal war. Finally, he pushes off the doorframe and walks to me. Dan opens the shower door, his half-lidded gaze raking over my fully naked and wet body, drinking in the sight.

Cool air rushes into the shower, making my nipples tighten. My breath shudders and a thrill of excitement races through me. I know he's seen me naked that one time before, perhaps another time if he watched me in the shower when I left the door open for him. But this is the second time we've been face to face like this, and I love the way he looks at me.

Dan's focus shifts to the rotating dildo on the shelf behind me. He presses a button on the remote and the machine switches off. "Did you like using it?"

I press my lips together and shake my head. "It hurt."

"You're a virgin. Of course it did."

"I think it was too big."

"I bet. You're tiny," he mutters. That same look of contemplation returns to his eyes as they rake over my body. "I am seriously going to hell for this."

"For what?"

Dan's dark gaze flicks up to mine, his voice rough. "Let me watch you use the dildo."

My eyes flare with shock and humility. My body has a different reaction, trembling with need. The ache in my pussy deepens, wanting this badly.

The softest chuckle leaves his lips. "You're shy all of a sudden?"

I know he's referring to the way I touched myself in front of him. All the times I'm alone in my bedroom and moan loud enough for him to hear what I'm doing to myself. Maybe even how I've showered with the bathroom door open. But using a dildo in front of Dan seems more intense. More... *wrong.*

It feels so much better when it's wrong.

A shiver of arousal rushes through me, making me realize how much I like the thought of Dan watching me use this toy. "I don't know how to use it properly."

"I'll teach you."

The delicate muscles between my legs flutter, remembering the last time we had a lesson like this. "It doesn't fit."

"You just need to warm up and take it slow. Are you wet?"

I nod.

"Suction it against the shower wall."

I chew my lip, equal parts confused and intrigued about what he has in mind. "How high?"

Dan takes the lead, suctioning the dildo down low, beneath my knee height. I stare at the thing, still confused about how I'm meant to use it at that height.

Reading my expression well, Dan directs me. "Get on all fours, Ally. Take it from behind. Most girls like it from that angle."

Some sick part of me gets off on the dominance he shows right now and me submitting to anything he says. I drop onto my hands and knees, my face to the shower entrance where Dan stands. He takes a few steps back, creating distance between us to give himself a better view of my face, and sits on the edge of the bathtub.

"Rub your clit. You're good at that from what I remember."

Following Dan's instructions, I hold myself up with one hand and touch my clit with the other, rubbing slow at first, my heart beating out of control. Being back in this scenario, where Dan teaches me what to do is exhilarating, and right from the start, I can feel my orgasm building.

"Good girl," Dan murmurs, watching every move I make. "Gently push back onto the dildo."

Aligning the tip to my opening, I sink back onto it, gasping as the head enters. The toy stretches me, but this time the pain isn't severe. It's hardly painful at all, instead a tight sensation now that I'm warmed up.

"That's it, Ally," Dan praises, his voice low. "Push back a little more. Let it stretch you open. It'll feel so much better once it's all the way in."

Slowly, I take the toy deeper until I gasp from the fullness, my pussy pressed to the hilt of the dildo. It's a feeling I've been craving for so long.

"Well done. Such a good listener, doing as you're told. Are you imagining it's my cock inside you?" Dan knows exactly what I need, and as I meet his gaze, I realize this moment isn't really about Dan teaching me to use a dildo. This is our way of having sex, of Dan fucking me and claiming my virginity. So to speak.

"Yes," I moan.

"Good. Start moving back and forth, nice and slow."

I do as he says, rocking on my hands and knees, adjusting to the dildo's size each time it fills me up. Little whimpers leave my lips. All pain is gone and I'm overcome with how good it feels to be wrapped around something so long and thick. My hips find their own rhythm, undulating over the shaft. With each movement I make, I hear the wet sounds of my pussy, and when I look up at Dan, my gaze catches on the erection jutting against his jeans.

"Now you're getting the hang of this." He presses a button on the remote, and I feel the toy start to vibrate inside me. The vibrations send a shockwave of pleasure through my body, into my clit, and I moan softly.

"Feel good, baby?" His voice is hoarse.

"Yes," I wince, trying not to be too loud.

"We're the only ones home. No need to hold back. You can be as loud as you need to." He presses another button, and I cry out as the head starts rotating, burrowing its way deeper inside me. "Fuck," he hisses, his eyes glued to my body. "Take it faster now."

I obey, picking up speed, my breath becoming shallow and ragged. I'm still damp from the shower and am now working up a sweat. My wet hair clings to my face and neck. I can feel an orgasm coiling deep within me, the sensation different from any orgasm I've experienced before. More intense. I'm desperate for it and chase the feeling, my ass slapping against the shower wall each time I impale myself on the dildo. The sight of me like this must be anything but pretty. I don't recognize myself at all. I don't care. I just need to come.

Dan marvels over the display I'm giving him. "Look how hard you're working. Clench your pussy like I taught you to."

I focus on his instruction, squeezing myself around the

dildo, moaning as I try to make my muscles as tight as possible.

"That's it. Feel how much more intense the pleasure is when your pussy has a dick to grip onto?"

I nod desperately, unable to talk.

"Do you like this, Ally, being on display for me? Doing filthy things you know you shouldn't?"

"Yes." He knows me so well.

"Could you just imagine if someone walked in on you right now and saw what a good girl you're being for your stepbrother?"

The pleasure of this toy is so much more intense than I ever expected. It's powerful and all-consuming, but it's Dan's words that makes my pussy quiver and clench tighter around the shaft.

"Squeeze harder, Ally. Come for me." Dan increases the vibrations yet again, sending me spiraling out of control.

I scream as my orgasm hits, my whole body trembling. Pleasure courses through me, leaving my senses reeling as I come harder than I ever have before. Dan presses another button, and I feel hot liquid spill inside me as the dildo ejaculates. Another cry leaves me, my muscles still contracting, refusing to let go of the pleasure that Dan has given me.

When the orgasm begins to ease, I pull away from the dildo, catching my breath on my hands and knees.

Dan's whisper cuts through the silence. "You'd take the real thing so much better than that toy."

Panting, I look up to find him approaching with slow steps. He crouches right in front of me, my skin heating all over again as he gently brushes my wet hair back from my forehead. He looks me over, studying my face with a tortured expression in his eyes. His finger hooks beneath my chin, tilting my face up to his.

"You're so pretty when you come, Ally," he whispers. "You've worked so hard. You must be exhausted. Let me clean you up."

Dan takes my arms, lifting me to my feet. He turns the shower on, the water warm and comforting, and detaches the shower head, silently washing the sweat off my body like I'm royalty and he worships me. I watch him, dazed and tingling with bliss. I'm in a dream I never want to leave.

His gaze moves lower, between my legs, and his jaw hardens. I realize the fake cum is leaking out of me. "I wish it was real," I murmur. "I wish it was yours. I wish we could be together. You're all I want."

Dan's eyes return to mine, dark and pained. He doesn't say anything, just takes a washcloth and wipes away the sticky liquid. He knows as well as I do that what I want can't happen. I don't let it ruin the moment.

In some sense, it truly does feel like Dan and I had sex tonight. Not physically, but he was in control of that toy and telling me how to use it. He's the one who gave me pleasure. It was the most vulnerable and intimate I've ever been, and it was with him.

When the water is switched off, Dan grabs a towel and wraps me in it, drying my hair and body. I expect him to leave now that we're done, like he did when teaching me how to touch myself, but he scoops me into his arms, cradling me like I'm a delicate doll, and carries me back to his bed.

Dan lays me beneath the covers, completely naked, then strips out of his own clothes, down to his boxers, and joins me in bed. He pulls me into his arms, his hard cock against my back, his hands cupping my breasts, and with his lips on the nape of my neck.

"This is all one-sided." My eyelids are heavy with the

call of sleep. "I want to see you without your clothes on. I want to see you come. *I* want to make you come."

"Not tonight. Sleep, my queen," he murmurs, his hot breath tickling my neck, his words giving me hope there'll be a next time. And I do fall asleep, the most content I've ever been in my life.

Chapter 16

Dan

There's no way I can fall asleep after what just happened between me and Ally in the bathroom. The things she lets me do to her...

Fuck.

I keep replaying the night in my mind as she sleeps tucked beneath my arm, where she belongs. The way she fucked that dildo, it was so raw and desperate. I can only imagine how she'd ride my cock. The sounds she made in that shower and the look on her face as she came... The memory will forever live in my head. I shouldn't have let any of it happen, but I'm in too deep, too consumed by this girl to feel even the slightest bit of guilt anymore.

I stroke her wet hair and kiss her cheek, my gaze traveling down the length of her naked body and enjoying every inch of what I see, her skin tinged blue beneath my neon lamp. I need to jerk off to get rid of this raging hard-on I have, but there's no way I can leave Ally's side. Tonight, it feels like she's truly mine, if only for a little while, and I won't waste a minute of it.

Tomorrow, things will be back to normal between us. We'll go about our day without addressing the events of tonight. It will be agony. I don't know how I'm meant to carry on living my life without... *fucking* Ally. Every single day. I need to be inside Ally and feel her come on my cock. I want to come inside her and be the only one who ever does. I want her to... *love* me, because I'm so madly in love with her.

There has to be some way we can be together, even if it's only in private. We've kept this attraction between us a secret for so long. Surely we can make something work.

In the morning, I'll tell her how I feel—that this isn't just about sex for me and I'm in love with her. I'm beyond caring about what's right or wrong, I just need her to be mine.

Chapter 17

Ally

The morning after, Saturday, June 2

The kiss

I wake in the morning, alone in Dan's bed. The dreamy haze from last night has worn off and my body is tender from my performance with that toy. Memories of the shower flash into my mind, and I'm flooded with embarrassment over how exposed and... *nasty* I got. I had no shame in that shower.

I sure as hell have shame right now. Not only was I acting like the star in a porno, but I enjoyed every second of it. The orgasm was the most intense thing I've ever experienced and it's all because I knew what Dan and I were doing was wrong. I got off on him watching me and the way he praised me, telling me I'm a good girl. I liked the power he had and that he was controlling the toy.

It's not just last night that's the issue. It's this obsession I have with him that makes me act differently—leaving the bathroom door open while I shower and hoping he'll watch me; when I'm alone in my bedroom touching myself, I moan a little louder so he can hear what I'm doing.

I don't recognize myself anymore. I don't know why I do the things I do. They feel good in the moment. They make me feel alive and powerful to be lusted after. Being the center of Dan's attention is intoxicating, and I keep pushing the boundaries, chasing the high it gives me.

I end up hating myself afterward, promising myself I'll never do it again. That this obsession with him will stop. That I won't crawl into his bed again. I won't finger myself to the thought of him. I won't leave the bathroom door open and let him watch the shower head give me an orgasm.

But it always happens again.

I'm an addict. A sex fiend. I feel dirty. If my mother and Josh ever found out about the things I do with Dan, I swear I would die. They see me as their sweet little daughter.

That's the girl I should be. As a Blackwood, I'm supposed to be a role model for Forever Families and display to the public how unified our blended family is.

Needing to shake this dirty feeling off, I return to my bedroom, dressing for the day. When I enter the living room, Mom and Josh are having their breakfast on the couch while discussing our upcoming departure for summer in The Hamptons. It's early June and we're traveling there in a week.

They say good morning to me without glancing my way, asking how I slept. My eyes snag on Dan in an armchair, shuffling the neon cards I bought him. I glance away, my cheeks blooming with color as I head for the kitchen. I feel his gaze follow me the entire time as I grab bread from the fridge and place it in the toaster.

"What are your plans for today, honey?" Mom asks, reading something on her phone.

"Um... I don't know." I can't think straight with Dan in the same room as me and give some dumb, flustered answer.

Dan laughs softly, like he knows I'm nervous because of him and last night. The next thing I know, he's right behind me, reaching over me to place his own bread in the toaster. I flinch away, then feel his warm hand on my lower back.

"You okay?" he whispers.

"Yeah. Why wouldn't I be?"

He studies me, his gaze soft. Amused. The left corner of his mouth lifts into that half grin I'm in love with. "No reason."

His hand on my lower back readjusts, slipping beneath my shirt and resting on my bare skin. I stiffen, my eyes whipping to our parents, realizing they're none the wiser. Regardless, that hand should *not* be there while we're in the same room as our parents. Or ever. I step away, reaching for the peanut butter.

"Oh, Ally, before I forget." Josh holds up a large envelope. "This arrived in the mail for you. It's from the Paris Conservatoire."

My interest sparks. It's probably a pamphlet. I signed up for the Conservatoire's mailing list a few months back. But I'm keen to read whatever is inside.

My toast pops. I spread the peanut butter, grab the envelope off Josh, and disappear into my room, eager to get away from Dan. Less than a minute later, I'm sitting on my bed and eating my breakfast when Dan enters my room, closing the door behind himself.

"Since when do you eat breakfast in your room?" he asks, mildly amused.

I shrug, not meeting his eyes. "Since today."

His voice loses the smug tone and is replaced with concern. "Was last night too much?"

No.

Yes.

"I liked it. Too much," I answer in a quiet voice, staring at my toast. "I feel guilty for liking it. I shouldn't have done that with you. I shouldn't do any of the things I do with you. It's wrong."

He doesn't say anything. I look up at him, seeing the sentiment of my words reflected in his eyes. He feels it too, that what we're doing is wrong. The only difference is there's no guilt in his eyes.

"What's in the envelope?" he asks.

"I don't know. Probably an advertisement."

"Open it."

I do, welcoming the change in subject.

Dear Alexandra Hastings,

We are pleased to inform you that you have been chosen as the recipient for the DeLacroix scholarship.

My heart stops and I reread the opening line several times, not understanding the words that are so clearly spelt out for me.

"What is this?" I step off the bed and hand the letter to Dan. "Is this a prank or something? I didn't apply for the scholarship."

He reads the letter, his mouth slowly rising into a grin. "Fuck, you actually got the scholarship. I *knew* you'd get it. I applied for you."

My hand claps to my mouth and I can feel my own smile forming. "I don't understand. How?"

"I took a video of you playing the piano when you weren't aware."

A short laugh of disbelief escapes me. And then the reality of the acceptance letter sinks in and I scream, jumping on the spot and bursting with excitement. From the corner of my eyes, I see Dan watching me, laughing.

"I can't believe you did this," I squeal. "Thank you, thank you, thank you. I love you."

I jump on him with all my weight. He stumbles backward, his legs bumping into my bed frame, and the two of us fall onto the mattress. My forehead thumps against Dan's as I land on top of him, and with it, the excitement of the moment shifts into something quiet when I realize I'm straddling him and how close our lips are. My hair forms a curtain down one side of our faces.

He's looking up at me with such amazement, proud of me for receiving the scholarship. And I realize in this moment that I'm in love with Dan. Not the excitable love I shouted about a moment ago, but true, deep love.

I think I've always loved him. I'm only recognizing the feeling now after he's done something so incredibly selfless for me. I love how supportive he is and how he believes in me. He takes time to learn about my interests. Socially, I've always struggled to fit in, but Dan has always liked who I am. He's always made me feel seen. He's my safe place.

Overall, he's just a good person. My *favorite* person. I love everything about him.

"Fuck it," Dan whispers, then presses up, his lips meeting mine for the first time ever.

The kiss is tender, catching me off guard and sending blissful sparks all through my body. I've been kissed before, once when I was younger, before meeting Dan. But I'd been tricked into thinking the guy liked me, later realizing the kiss had been a dare.

This, right now with Dan, feels like the first real kiss I've ever had, and it's perfect.

I pull back, studying Dan's eyes, confused as to how we've done so much together, yet a simple kiss can feel so magical and intimate. Despite everything I said a moment ago, about how we're wrong, I want more. That's the way it goes with Dan. I always want more, no matter how much I shouldn't.

Between my legs, I feel how hard Dan is from the kiss. I grind against his dick, letting out a tiny moan at the tenderness I still have from last night, mixed with the pleasure that spreads within me.

Dan flips me on my back, getting me beneath him, and kisses me harder this time, pinning me to the mattress with his lips. His dick grinds against me, like he's fucking me, and I move with him, sliding my tongue inside his mouth.

"Ally, baby, you have no idea how much I love—"

"Honey?" Mom knocks on the door, the wall muffling her voice. "What happened? I heard you screaming."

Dan and I push a part, right before the door opens and my mom steps inside. She looks at us, a mix of concern and curiosity in her eyes.

I grab the acceptance letter before I have a chance to look guilty and jump off the bed, handing it to her. "Dan applied to the Paris Conservatoire for me in secret. I just got accepted into that DeLacroix scholarship I was telling you about."

She reads the letter with just as much disbelief as I had. Her face lights up the farther down the page she reads, and then she's hugging me eagerly, speaking words of congratulations.

"Dan, you did this for Ally? You are *so* incredible. Come on, we have to tell Josh." Mom grabs my hand and rushes me out of my room to where I left Josh only minutes ago, sitting on the couch with his breakfast. "Your son applied to the Paris Conservatoire in secret for Ally and she just received her acceptance letter."

Josh looks between me and Dan who is now standing behind me. "You got in? That's amazing." He hugs me just as my mother did, and I get lost in the moment, filled with excitement. "Ally, this is so incredible. When do you need to leave for Paris? How long is the scholarship for?"

The logistics of Josh's question stunts my excitement. Until now, all that's crossed my mind is exhilaration that I'm a good enough musician to receive the scholarship. But this scholarship was never my plan A. Accepting the scholarship would entail moving to Paris and leaving my family behind. Leaving *Dan* behind. I'd be in a new city by myself. I've never done anything like this on my own. What if I'm alone in Paris and have a panic attack and can't calm myself down?

I chew my bottom lip, suddenly overwhelmed with confusion. Even apprehension. "I don't know if I'll accept the scholarship."

"What?" Mom and Josh gasp at the same time.

"Ally, you have to," Mom says. "This is an incredible opportunity."

"I know. And I'm grateful Dan did this for me, but... moving to Paris is a big deal. I'd be alone and... What if I don't cope?"

"I already thought this through when I applied," Dan says. "You don't have to accept the scholarship if you don't want to. I won't be offended. I only applied to it because I wanted you to have options. If location is the only thing holding you back, I'll move to Paris with you. I can easily play poker there."

The look in Dan's eyes as he says those words is so sincere. But I can't tell which Dan is speaking them. The Dan who is my best friend? My stepbrother? The guy who likes teaching me how to enjoy my body? Or the guy who held me in his arms last night, kissing my forehead as I fell asleep?

It's a rude reminder that I shouldn't be in love with him. If we move to Paris together, this thing between us will only grow more out of hand. We'll be together like an actual couple, not having to carefully tread around the family and public like we do now. I'll fall more in love with him. We'll have sex. We'll be even more tangled up in each other and it will be a mess. A complete disaster that will end in heartbreak because there's no future for me and Dan.

I take a steadying breath and glance out the window, anywhere but at Dan. "Um... My mind is chaos right now. I think I'd like to spend a few days with Uncle Daxton just to talk things through."

"Of course, sweetie," Mom says. "I'll call him right now. He'll love to have you stay with him."

"I'm going to pack a bag." I head to my room and grab a small suitcase from my wardrobe, throwing a bunch of clothes in it.

"You okay?" Dan asks, closing the door behind himself.

I don't stop to look at him, knowing if I do, I'll want to kiss him again. I'll tell him I love him, and I can't do that. "Yeah, just what I said—I need to think things through. Paris is a big decision."

"And you need to be away from me to think things through." He says it as a statement, though I can hear the displeasure in his voice.

I sigh, continuing to pack clothes. "I love that you got the scholarship for me. You're perfect, Dan. Beyond perfect. But you shouldn't have kissed me."

He laughs, the sound bitter. "The way you're acting makes me feel anything but perfect. Of all the things we've done, kissing was crossing the line?"

"It wasn't just the kiss. But yes, it was crossing the line because it was physical. It scares me."

Aside from sharing a bed and falling asleep in each other's arms, we haven't technically done anything sexual *together*. It's all been from a distance and we've barely acknowledged any of it. Somehow, that distance and lack of acknowledgement has given me a sense of comfort, like I'm not truly crossing the line with Dan. There's been a barrier between us and now that barrier is gone.

I love Dan and there's a desperate need in me to give all of my mind and body over to him. It's wrong and I wish I didn't feel this way about Dan. I wish things were simple and I wasn't filled with so much shame for loving him.

"I just need space to think. This scholarship has come out of the blue. We'll talk in a few days, okay?" I zip up the suitcase and wheel it out of my room, right past Dan without looking at him to maintain my sanity.

Chapter 18

Dan

Five days later, Thursday, June 7
QUEEN OF HEARTS

Felix owns an apartment on the Upper East Side and I've been crashing at his place for the last five days while Ally stays with her uncle. There's always a party taking place here. Felix has people over every night. There's constant drinking and drugs. Music is always playing. People sleep on the floor. They fuck in the bedrooms. I've even seen them fuck outside the bedrooms, not caring about privacy. It's chaotic, but I can't stay at home, not when everything about the place reminds me of Ally.

She hasn't spoken to me in five days.

She said she wants space to clear her head. I'm respecting her wishes, but these have become the most painful five days of my life, waiting for her to reach out to me.

I can't help but think I ruined everything with that one kiss. We had a dynamic and I changed it. But I couldn't stop myself from kissing her. Ally looked so damn happy receiving the scholarship acceptance letter. It might be the happiest I've ever seen her. I lost control and kissed her. A kiss I've waited four fucking years to have.

She grinded against me, so desperate to feel my dick between her legs. Ally would have let me fuck her right then and there, regardless that we weren't home alone. How quickly it all turned to shit. I've never seen anyone pack their bags so fast, all to put distance between us. She couldn't even look at me.

"Bro, what the hell is with you tonight?" Felix speaks over the music, taking a seat beside me on the couch in his living room. He has a Jack Daniel's in one hand. With the other, he pulls a blond in a bikini onto his lap. "A better question would be what is with you *every* night? You're not drinking or getting any pussy. You're miserable every day."

"Nothing is wrong. I'm just not in the mood." I'd been out on the balcony with everyone a moment ago, the only one fully dressed and not sitting in the hot tub, but had enough when two people started having sex in the water.

"Girl problems?"

"No. It's nothing."

"She not into you or something?" Felix pushes. "Got a boyfriend?"

"It's not about a girl. Dad is pissing me off more than normal."

"Ah, makes sense now, why you're acting so lovesick over our father." He laughs. The girl takes his hand, guiding him to his bedroom. He calls back to me, "Seriously, have a drink. Fuck some pussy. Problem solved."

There was a time when that solution would have

worked. Now, I can't bear the thought of being with anyone other than Ally.

Being at Felix's place with the many girls that approach me is only making everything worse. I grab my keys and leave the apartment, getting into my car and driving around the city to clear my head. But the only clarity the drive gives me is that I need Ally by my side. She's scared, but we can talk through her fears. We can keep what we have private and make this work between us. No one has found out about our feelings this far.

I drive to Ally's uncle's building—the hotel Ally used to live in before our parents got married—deciding I'm going to confess everything to her. I'll tell her how much she means to me, that I adore her, fucking *love* her, and that I don't care if we're wrong together on paper.

When I enter the lobby, I call Ally's phone, not surprised when she doesn't answer. I approach the front desk, seeking out the receptionist. "I need to get a message to the penthouse. My... A family member is visiting—"

"The residents of the penthouse are out of town on business," a male receptionist tells me. "They left this morning."

"Did they mention whether their niece was staying behind?"

"Ah, Ally. No, she departed this morning, too."

I return to my car, driving home with the hopes of finding Ally there. The night is late. She wouldn't be anywhere else.

It's not long before I step through the front door, finding Dad alone on the couch, watching a news station.

"You're home," he says as I walk by him for my bedroom. "How was your time with Felix?"

"Fine. Not really in the mood for chitchat. I need to talk to Ally about something."

"Ally?" The confusion in his voice is enough to stop me in my tracks. "Ally and Amabella left today."

"Left? Where did they go?"

He scrunches his nose with even more confusion. "Paris. I thought you knew this."

Paris?

My heart sinks and I have this awful feeling in my stomach. I *can't* be hearing my father right. How could Ally be in Paris already when the scholarship doesn't start for another few months? Why is Amabella with her?

Ally hasn't said goodbye to me. She hasn't said *anything* at all.

My throat closes up. I work hard to swallow down the disbelief and sickness rising in me. "Oh, right. I did know. I got my dates mixed up. I haven't been sober for the last five days. You know what it's like when I get together with Felix."

My father scowls. His judgment is the last thing I care about right now.

"You should call Ally," he says, flicking through the TV channels. "I'm worried about her. She came home from Daxton's with this frantic urge to get to Paris immediately. Amabella insisted she travel with Ally for the first week to help get her settled into her new home. I would have gone too but there are work meetings I can't get out of." He starts talking about Forever Families. I don't hear a word of it. Nothing registers except when he says, "Ally said she left something for you on your bed."

My heart races, needing to find whatever Ally left me. There has to be some explanation for her behavior. Some misunderstanding that's about to be cleared up. She wouldn't leave me like this. There'll be a plane ticket with my name on it waiting on my bed.

She wouldn't just leave.

I excuse myself and enter my room. And there it is, an envelope on my bed. I rip the paper open, searching for that plane ticket. A handwritten letter waits for me instead.

Dan,

This thing between us has grown out of control. When I received the scholarship acceptance letter, I realized something that scares me.

I'm in love with you, Dan.

I love you so much it hurts. Having you in my life is the best thing that has ever happened to me. But I can't be in love with you. Our relationship is wrong in every sense and sooner or later someone will discover us. I can't bear to think of what others would say. My mother and Josh would be disgusted. If this leaked to the public, it's not only our lives that would be impacted. The family reputation would be destroyed. Forever Families would never recover.

I've had a lot of time to think during the past few days, and I've come to the realization that I will never stop loving you if we continue the way we are. I'm accepting the scholarship in Paris as a chance to start fresh, where I can try to move on with my life.

I'm sorry for leaving without saying goodbye. You deserve a proper goodbye in person, but I knew I could never make myself go through with this plan if I saw you again. I knew you wouldn't let me go, because I think maybe you love me too. You need to let go of me, Dan. We both need to move on from each other.

Please, don't follow me to Paris, and please don't contact me at all. When I return, I promise I'll return as your friend and sister and nothing more.

Please don't hate me for doing this. And please, destroy this letter as soon as you've read it. No one can ever know about us.

Ally,

xxoo

My chest is in agony as I read the letter. My lungs constrict and I can barely breathe. Her reasoning is understandable, and yet I'm angry. So fucking angry at Ally for leaving like this after everything we've been through and all that I've done for her. The worst part is I never got the chance to tell Ally how much I love her.

I'm about to scrunch the envelope but realize something else is inside it. I pull it out, finding the Queen of Hearts card I gave Ally. Words are written across the black card in white ink. Ally's handwriting. *You'll always be my person.*

The words burn my eyes. My chest aches like nothing I've ever felt before. She said she'd never let go of this card.

Fucking liar.

I love her. Yet I hate her for being a coward and running away. How could she do this to me. To *us*. I kick my bed frame, swearing and clawing both hands through my hair.

My phone beeps with a text message. I check it, foolish for hoping it's from Ally.

FELIX

Bro, you left the party. Get back here.
Booze and pussy makes everything better.
Promise.

Fuck. I need a distraction from how much this hurts.

I place Ally's letter and the Queen of Hearts in my bedside drawer and stand from my bed, leaving my room and heading straight back to Felix's apartment where I can drink and meet a new girl who helps me forget all about the one who has ripped my heart straight from my chest.

TO BE CONTINUED

Find out what happens next for Ally and Dan in book 1 of the Playing Favorites series, MY FAVORITE SIN.

Turn the page to read the **first chapter** of My Favorite Sin.

BOOKS BY SKYLA SUMMERS

Celebrity Fake Dating series
Fake Dating Adrian Hunter (enemies to lovers)
Fake Dating Zac Delavin (grumpy/sunshine)
Fake Dating Daxton Hawk (pen pals)

Playing Favorites series
My Favorite Girl
My Favorite Sin

To stay up to date with my latest book news, sign up to my monthly newsletter at **www.skylasummers.com** or follow me on **Instagram: @authorskylasummers**

REVIEWS AND SPREADING THE WORD
Book reviews are invaluable to an author's success. If you enjoyed this book, leaving a written review and star rating on the *My Favorite Girl* Amazon and Goodreads page will be much appreciated. Spreading the word via any social media platforms you may have is also greatly appreciated.

MY FAVORITE SIN

Chapter 1

DAN

I lost five hundred thousand dollars playing poker earlier today because all I could think about during the game was that time Ally fingered herself in front of me.

I think about that night often, among others which never should have happened between us. She was always so caught up on being a good girl in front of our parents and the public's eyes. Behind closed doors she was *my* good girl.

The things she did in front of me were filthy. And yet the one time I kissed her, she ran scared, fleeing from New York to Paris for a year without saying goodbye to me.

She thought a hand-written letter would be an adequate goodbye. While I wait in the terminal for her flight to disembark, I read Ally's letter again. The paper is crumpled from how many times I've studied her words.

I'm in love with you, Dan.

I can't be in love with you. Our relationship is wrong in every sense.

Fuck. I was in love with her too but never got the chance to tell her.

Who am I kidding, I'm *still* in love with her. I thought I could stay angry with Ally for leaving the way she did. I thought I could get over her. But this year apart has changed nothing for me. I'm more obsessed with her now than ever. I don't care that my father married her mother.

When I return from Paris, I promise I'll return as your friend and nothing more.

Passengers start trickling out of the arrivals gate. I tuck Ally's letter into the inside pocket of my jacket and rest one shoulder against the wall while waiting for my girl to appear.

My mind wanders to curiosities about Ally and all the ways she'll have changed from the girl I knew. Will she have moved on from me like she intended to? Is there someone new in her life? Is she still a virgin?

That last question... My jaw clenches at the thought of anyone touching Ally. Perhaps it's best I don't find out the answer.

It's not long before I spot her among the crowd of passengers. My pulse is thumping so fucking loud in my ears I can't hear a damn thing inside this airport. The sight of her has me burning up like I'm a teenager again and about to have sex for the first time. How the fuck is Ally more beautiful than the last time I saw her?

How am I supposed to act like nothing happened between us?

Some guy—another passenger, I assume—is chatting her up as they walk with the flow of people. I can't blame him for being interested in her. She has this alluring presence like she's not even from this world. The first time I saw Ally she was fifteen, I was a year older, and she looked like some creature that had stepped out of a mythical story. A nymph or a fairy. So incredibly gorgeous.

The Ally in front of me still has that vibe. Her hair is the palest blond, slung over one shoulder and trailing down to her waist. Her complexion matches, as though she's never stepped foot in the sun. She has the prettiest lips. And those goddamn eyes that constantly say *fuck me*... I swear they're the brightest blue any eyes have ever been.

Her fashion hasn't changed. Always pastels and whites and like she belongs in a country garden. She's wearing a yellow dress with a delicate pink flower pattern and sleeves that fall off her shoulders. The bodice hugs her tits, which I shouldn't take notice of, but there's no ignoring how incredible her cleavage is. A pink satin ribbon sits in her hair. Always the ribbons and bows, like she's a little girl instead of twenty.

The urge to announce myself is strong. I want to wrap Ally in my arms. Lift her off her toes and spin her in circles. I need to see her smile at me and hear her sweet voice.

I hold off, unsure of our dynamic. I'm not certain she'll be pleased to see I'm the one picking her up from the airport.

Remaining in my spot, I lean against the wall and watch Ally walk with this guy. He looks to be the same age as us, clean cut and with a smile that lets me know he's into her. They come to a standstill. As I've seen so many times before, Ally starts fidgeting with her hair and shifts back and forth on her feet. Her shoulders grow tight. Her smile is strained. The guy makes eye contact with Ally and her gaze drops to the floor.

She's still awkward around new people, that much hasn't changed.

Ally holds her hand out to shake, forcing an end to their

interaction. The guy looks down at her palm, a little confused, then shakes it and leaves. I can't help but laugh over how adorably awkward Ally can be sometimes. I shouldn't feel so relieved by the guy's dismissal. It's not like I can have Ally for myself.

Ally scans the terminal for our parents. My heart pounds so heavily I can feel it as her gaze grows closer and closer to my direction until... Those blue eyes pause on me. We're staring at each other for what feels like a lifetime. I can't move. I can't seem to make myself do anything.

Her cheeks turn rosy beneath my gaze. Then suddenly she's... *smiling* at me. It's small, but the smile is there, and I'm so relieved that she's pleased to see me.

Ally steps up to me and lowers her carry-on luggage to the ground before wrapping her arms around my neck. The hug is guarded. She doesn't get too close and keeps distance between our bodies.

I should follow Ally's lead, but this moment feels surreal, too good to be true, and I pull her close, afraid she'll disappear. Ally laughs softly, caught off guard by my actions, but doesn't pull away. The sound of her voice is heaven. I breathe in Ally's floral scent and hug her tighter. I want to feel her lips beneath mine so fucking badly and remember what she tastes like.

I notice something else that makes me frown. She's tiny in my arms. Tinier than I remember. Ally hasn't been taking care of herself. What about her panic attacks? I've often worried about her mental health, being alone in a foreign country.

With reluctance, I end the hug, not knowing how to greet her.

I missed you.

I've thought about you every day.

You broke my heart, leaving the way you did.

None of those options seem appropriate. "How was your flight?"

"Fine." Her voice is cautious. She stands in silence, her gaze roaming my face, her expression troubled. "You look really different, like you've been hanging around Felix too much."

In other words, I've lost the boyish look of jeans and hoodies and replaced them with suits. I *have* been hanging around my oldest brother a lot, ever since Ally left. The parties are non-stop. So are the poker games and visits to his speakeasy. Felix was bound to rub off on me.

"What are you doing here?" Ally asks. "I thought our parents were picking me up."

"They had a last-minute work thing to take care of and called me to be here instead."

"Okay. No problem. Should we get out of here?"

"Sure." I pick up Ally's carry-on luggage and sling it over my shoulder.

"I can carry that." There's apprehension in her voice. Perhaps I shouldn't be carrying her belongings; it's something a boyfriend would do.

As I pass the bag back to Ally, a camera flash goes off nearby, making her jolt. Several more flashes light up our surroundings. Neither us bother searching for the photographer. It's been ingrained in us as offspring of a high-profile marriage to ignore paparazzi. But Ally still hates it.

Our parents are known for their philanthropic ways and five years ago, when they got engaged, they founded Forever Families, a charity to assist families in need. They've thrown it upon our family that we're to be the face of the foundation, portraying how a blended family can be a strong unit. I think it's great they're so passionate about helping others. I just don't want to be a part of it, not when my father has been absent for the majority of my life, and all I ever want to do is get Ally naked. Nor do I want to live my life walking around on eggshells to aid the family image.

"Best part about Paris—no one took my photo."

"Walk on this side of me," I tell Ally, placing myself between her and the camera.

I've never cared about the public attention as much as she has. When I was younger, sometimes I enjoyed it. But I can't say I'm looking forward to today's poker loss hitting the news. Ally, on the other hand, stresses over what the tabloids say about her, always wanting to uphold a good reputation for our parents and Forever Families.

Of course, she never does anything scandalous for the tabloids to report on. At least, nothing anyone knows of, except me. A relationship with me would definitely not be accepted by the public. The last I heard, the media were praising Ally for how talented and dedicated she is to her piano studies at the Paris Conservatoire.

"So, what's the plan for tonight?" Ally asks as we follow the stream of people heading for the luggage collection area. "Mom told me she and Josh are still living in the beach house. You're not driving me to The Hamptons at this hour, are you?"

"I thought you could spend a couple of days with me in the city before I take you to our parents."

Her cheeks darken and she licks her lips, keeping her eyes straight ahead of us. "Sure, that sounds like fun."

My suggestion makes her uncomfortable. The invitation to stay at my place is innocent. Despite still being in love with this girl, I've missed having her as my friend this last year. Friendship was the start of our relationship, five years ago when our parents introduced us. From the color in Ally's cheeks right now, I can tell she's thinking about all the times we were more than just friends and that staying at my place will be dangerous.

"I can take you to our parents straight away, if you prefer," I tell her as we step onto the escalator, descending to the ground floor.

"No, don't hassle yourself. It will be good to spend some time in the city."

"If you're sure."

Our conversation is stilted and unnatural. She's being awkward around me, and I hate it. One of the things I love most about Ally is how she's shy around most people except me. She has to be nervous over the way things ended with us. I don't know how to broach the topic or if I even should. Maybe it's best I don't mention the past.

Ally and I rarely spoke about the inappropriate things we used to do. The silence gave her a sense of comfort. It was her way of pretending like she wasn't doing anything wrong. Is she going to run away all over again if I ask to talk about the past? I can't risk that, not when I've just got her back.

"So, tell me everything about Paris."

She smiles again, and this time when she talks, the Ally I used to know reappears—the girl who used to talk my ear off for hours on end about her passion for music. Her voice rises in pitch and speed as she launches into a recap of her year abroad. "DeLacroix was such a phenomenal piano teacher. I learned the most amazing things from him. Performed in the most amazing cathedrals. I got to visit so many incredible historical places. Dan, I stood where Debussy stood. It was so surreal to be where these famous composers once were. A dream come true."

"Did you visit the Catacombs?"

She rolls her eyes at my teasing and gives a laugh of disapproval as we arrive at the baggage collection. "You know that's illegal."

"Wouldn't have stopped me."

"I visited Saint-Saëns's grave and Chopin's tomb. Does that count? It was so beautiful but also sad. I shed a few tears."

Of course she did. I chuckle at the information, relieved that some sense of normality has returned between us.

"I'm being weird, aren't I? Sorry," she says. "You probably don't care about any of these details."

I have no interest in this classical music stuff whatsoever, aside from the fact that Ally loves it. So, naturally, it's become a passion of mine too.

"You *know* I care about these details. I want to hear everything. Ally..." A confession sits on the tip of my tongue. Against the warning in my head, I say the words out loud. "I missed you. I thought about you a lot—"

"Oh, there's my suitcase." Ally points to the conveyor belt and leaves my side.

She heard me. I know she did. She's setting a precedent. Ally has moved on from me, just like she promised in her letter.

I'm the only one between us who is still plagued with this obsession.

Acknowledgments

Thank you to my beta readers, editor, cover designer, ARC readers, and everyone who has taken part in hyping up this story.

Thank **you** for reading this story.

The biggest thank you goes to my husband. I'd be a starving artist without him. Actually, I wouldn't be writing at all and would be instead hating my life as a teacher. He is the most incredible and supportive husband and is the whole reason this book is in your hands. I love him to pieces!

About the Author

Skyla Summers is an Australian author who lives with her husband and daughter in the sunny state of Queensland. Her favorite part of story telling is making characters fall in love. She always enjoys talking with her readers.

You can message Skyla through her website www.skylasummers.com or find her on social media. **Instagram: @authorskylasummers.**

Printed in Great Britain
by Amazon